The Reunion
The Sequel to Rachel's Forbidden Love

A Novel by

Lucy Heath

ISBN: 1490546529
ISBN 13: 9781490546520
Cover Illustrations by: Dee Boyd

Dedication:

To faithful readers who still believe in romance and Christian courtship —

Thanks

To family members and friends who inspired me toward character development

God moves in a mysterious way

His wonders to perform; He plants

His footsteps in the sea

And rides upon the storm

— William Cowper

To: The Clarkscoder Family
Thanks for your Support.

Love
LOCK

Prologue

Most of the *People* in the district did not know why the bishop, my husband's brother, set us aside for a *'proving'*. They certainly did not know, and hopefully did not suspect anything about our daughter's secret marriage to Robert. That happened almost four years ago, this coming March. To think that at that time she also carried the burden of expecting *'wee'* ones by a husband that no one knew about, and who had seemingly vanished from the face of the earth. Well, it's more than I can do to thank the good *Lord Heavenly Father*, for a young girl to have the kind of faith that Rachel had. I dare say it wasn't just our Rachel with problems. I thank the good Lord also for my husband who stood strong, and firm in our *new found* faith as Christians. He would not recant, or deny that we now believed in salvation through Christ. So, for that reason, we had to suffer the full reproof of the *'Bann'*. Even with being *shunned* we were not without friends. Some of the *People* (the name we give to those of the Amish community), who we had known and loved over the years, found ways to stay in touch with us. There was always the U.S. mail, or by what we called 'root' letters *letters that travel from house to house, or from family to family by post, or by hand delivered drop-offs. Root letters carried news of the latest family events, things happening in the Amish community, or just plain old gossip.*

Just like the youth did for their courting, we would hint as to where we would be on a certain day, and time, just in case of accidentally meeting up with each other. We still had our good neighbors, the Millers, (now, secretly related to us by our daughter's marriage to their nephew) and there was my own sister. Mary and her husband Jesse Esh are Mennonite, so the *'Bann'* really did not affect them; nor did it apply to my other daughter, Elizabeth and her husband Ben, who left the Amish church a few years back.

They had a 'wee' one about two and a half years ago, and I'm so thankful that we can visit with them, and they can visit us. However, I'm a little more challenged when it comes to visiting my dear sister-in-law, Mae Zook. Ya see; Mae is the bishop's wife, and the bishop is my husband Daniel's brother. But, all things considered, that's one of those sly little things I told you about. Either Mae, or I would arrange to pay a visit with my sister Mary, and one of us would just *happen by*, and before you knew it, there you were... having a good old fashioned visit. Those meetings were welcomed, but they still didn't fill the void and sting of being shunned. We have our salvation in the Lord, but that doesn't mean we don't have feelings, and that we know for sure that Shunning is a hurtful thing. And, just because we've decided to live for Christ, doesn't mean we've gone all out to be *English* either. When one comes from such strict Amish customs, and upbringings, it takes time to adjust to certain liberties. We don't intend to give up, or change everything about our lifestyle, because most of what we adhere to is strongly based in the Bible. For instance, the 'Old Order' Amish hold strict to the commandment of "...*no graven images*', so for that reason we don't take any pictures, or have family photos of each other. We are taught to view the beauty of God in all men.

I have often asked forgiveness for letting my feelings of sadness, and misfortune about the Shunning surface so much, when my very own daughter Rachel, carries so many more hardships. Ach, (*a response that can mean: yes, well, wow, heaven's yes, etc.*) when she first heard of Robert's disappearance she was secretly married to him, and expecting babies. She was only sixteen years old for pity sakes! That was a terribly hard thing for her to come and tell us, but we were so thankful that she too had come to know the Lord, and He gave her the solace she needed to see her through to where she is today.

So many things have changed since those dark, dreadful days when Rachel had to give up her babies. She has moved from the '*Dawdi Haus*', (a smaller dwelling attached to the family house) back into the main house with the rest of the family, and still has hope of her husband's return someday. So, I'll try not to fret over what God will, and can do. It's not for me to judge...I just have to trust and believe in His divine Will for her life, and for ours too.

Prayer does change things. I have to admit that God has great compassion for His people. Sometimes we would honor Him with our prayers and our lips, but our hearts were not in what we said. Oh, I don't mean to say that we were being hypocrites; it's just that even in our constant belief, the light of hope would sometimes flicker and dim in our hearts. How often did we hope in these past few years that the Millers would rush over to the farm to bring glad news of Robert's return, but that has not happened? They too, keep waiting for an official phone call, or letter from the Army saying he has been found.

How does one hang on to hope when people look at you and say one thing, but looking pass their faces into their eyes, you can almost see them shaking their heads, and shucking their teeth saying, *...poor Rachel, such a pity. What a terrible thing to happen to such a young, sweet girl. Ach,* they probably look at the entire Zook household in that manner, but I know one thing: *for sure, and for certain!* God is a God of promise, and the end has not yet been seen.

chapter

ONE

I remember how happy I was the morning after my secret marriage and honeymoon night with Robert. He was leaving for Boot Camp that next day. Daed had given Robert permission to court me when he returned from his basic training in the Army, but what my family, and his did not know, is that we had been courting already. In the Amish community, parents allow their 'come of age' youth to begin dating if they desire. At age sixteen through age twenty-one we get freedom to experience our *"Rumschpringe"(the running around years)*. We are allowed to experience the outside world (so to speak) to see what it has to offer us. We also attend what we call *'Singings'*. These are mostly held on the Sunday evening at the house that hosted the Sunday service. The Amish keep with the tradition of having church services in their homes. The neighbor who hosted the meeting would see that his barn was swept and cleaned. Things were moved aside in order to make room for the young people who wanted to come back that evening for the Singing. This was for those youth in their Rumschpringe, or for those who just wanted to have an evening out away from their parents. The host house provided food for the gathering, and mainly, we would sit at the long picnic tables in the swept out barn to sing songs from the Ausbund (the Amish hymnal). After the night dwindled on, a fellow who might have his eye on a special girl would get up enough nerve to mosey on over to her, and strike up a conversation. If they hit it off, they would pair up for the evening, in hopes of leaving together in his courting buggy. If all went well, they would probably become a couple. If either of them could tell after their first courting that neither was the type of person they wanted to continue to date, he, or she would receive a letter that relayed that message. It's kind of a good way to do things, because by the time the next singing came around, they wouldn't be expecting to pair up with you as a couple, and you could be free to look for someone else. Of course, there were other ways of meeting someone special, but going to a 'Singing' was one of the main traditions for meeting a future mate. The idea being, that you would meet your spouse to be; take your lifelong kneeling vows to the Amish church, and therefore live happily ever after.

'Ach', the problem with that was, I never met the beau who was right for me; that is, until I realized it was Robert, and I sure didn't meet him at a 'Singing'. When I first realized I had feelings for him, and he had feelings for me, everything would have been just fine, except for two little issues: One; he was not Amish. He was what the Amish call an *Englischer, (most Americanized people outside of the Amish faith),* and two; he was a Negro. I had seen Robert on many times whenever I visited with Tina Marie, his cousin. He had come to live with Mr. and Mrs. Miller who owned the property next to ours. Their daughter, Tina Marie, and I, over the years, had become very good friends. As a matter of fact, several years ago, we became closer than most Amish girlfriends. But, that wasn't a strange thing, because for almost as long as I could remember, the Millers had always owned that property. Never in all my days did I ever think, or imagine I would have feeling for her cousin Robert, *in that way.* It all came falling on me that night he rescued me from a disastrous situation with an Amish boy I went on a date with.

☙❧

Rachel sat, reflecting back on what had taken place that night, and than her thoughts moved to the day of her and Robert's secret marriage, and the night of their honeymoon. That next day she had been invited to ride with his family to the train station to see Robert off. However, as far as the family knew, they had invited her along as his intended fiancée *to be*, not as his wife!

Rachel did not want to say her goodbye openly to Robert, in a public place. The Amish were not ardent to a display of open affection in public places, besides, how would it look anyway for a Negro guy (or any guy) and an Amish girl (dressed in full traditional garb) to be showing intimate affection in a parking lot? She remembered thinking, *suppose he wants to kiss me. For pity sakes! The stares we would get.* Rachel was thankful his family wanted to say their goodbyes to him inside the depot. She remembered how guilty she felt that everyone, but Tina, thought she was saying goodbye to her beau, but she was really saying goodbye to her husband. Not knowing the months of anguish that lay ahead for her at that time, Rachel was often convinced that God was punishing her for being so disobedient, and taking matters into her own hands. But, at other times she was convinced that no matter what the cost; it was God's prompting that led her to make the decision she did on that day.

Bearing a secret even more terrible than my marriage to Robert, I had just one more weeks to wait until his return home from Basic Training; then he could tell my Daed that we were married, and I could tell my husband that we were expecting a *'wee'* one. But, that day never came. Three days before he was to come back home, we got news that he was involved in a terrible incident. His unit commanders informed the Millers that they pieced together as much information as they could, and although they had recovered some of his personal belongings, Robert had not been found. It was as if he just vanished from the face of the earth. After thorough investigations on their part, and with the help of local authorities, they still came up empty. Though the case would not be closed, the training camp finally sent his personal belongings home to the only family they knew he had, Ezekiel, and Norma Jean Miller.

For the next two years, everything seemed to go by in a blear; the shunning of my parents, though not directly because of what the bishop called 'my wayward' ways. Having babies that I could never hold in my arms, and the anguish of longing for a husband I may never see again was beyond punishment for anyone, let alone for a sixteen-year-old girl. Now at age nineteen, I had to live the life of a widow, and the ways of a *'maidel', (a girl who has never been married)*. I watched my baby being loved by another family who literately lived at my front door, and I couldn't do a thing about it. I thanked God for the small circle of support that I did have: Mamm, Daed, Elizabeth and her husband Ben, the Millers, also uncle and Aendi Esh. I often thought of Tina Marie, and the devotion she had in keeping my secret. That must have been a terrible thing to go through alone. She really is a good sister-friend. There were other life long friends of the family, who though the Bann kept them from associating with us in the natural, prayed for us constantly. The Amish may not have prayed their prayers aloud, like some of us do now, but the power of their faith in God still reached our spirits. I appreciate everything that is being done to help my present situation, but sometimes it just doesn't seal the cracks in my broken heart, or the emptiness of barren arms. *"Oh God, where is my beloved Robert, and when will I ever hold my precious babies again?"*

During those first couple of years, one of the hardest things to do was to remain true to the adoption agreement with the Zimmerman's. Meanwhile, between cousin Ruthie's little girl, Rosie Ann, and Elizabeth's baby boy, 'Little Ben', I got the chance to cuddle babies, smother them with sweet kisses, and do a little babysitting. They didn't even mind letting me spoil the 'wee' ones a little. When I began to feel stronger, I moved back in with Daed, and Mamm, to stay in my old bedroom, but the 'Dawdi Haus' was always an option for a place of refuge.

When tragedy strikes a family in the Amish community, it affects all the People. That's what happened when Laverna Zimmerman's illness suddenly resurfaced. She had gone along for the past two and a half years, or so, seemingly making great progress in her health, then out of nowhere; she became violently ill, and had to be hospitalized. Within a couple of days, her husband was told that everything had been done to save her life, but it had been too late. It was surmised by the doctors that Laverna must have had many warning signs to indicate how severe the reoccurring illness had become, but for some reasons, she didn't take heed. Later, Mr. Zimmerman said he thought it was because she thought that if she had to be hospitalized for some length of time, they would take the baby away from her. During those few days, he never left her side. Their relatives in Lancaster, Pa. were notified of her grave illness. They were going to come in to take care of Robert Jr., but before they could get to Walnut Creek, Laverna was gone. Then, they were needed more than ever.

Mrs. Lapp looked after the baby while Mr. Zimmerman stayed at the hospital. When he returned to the house, she allowed her daughter, Nellie to help out. Everyone was heavy with grief at Laverna's passing, but not as obvious as poor Zack. So far as my parents were concerned, Uncle bishop could not lift the *Bann*, so they could not attend the funeral services for Mrs. Zimmerman, or the gathering afterwards, because both things were held in her home. But, they could pay their respects privately after everyone else had gone. The shunning would not allow them to associate with other *'freinds'* (Pennsylvania Dutch for 'friends) in any public setting. However, the bishop was not completely without sympathy. He agreed to my parent's visit, but made it clear that this was a one time thing, and not to be continued.

From that point on things began to move along differently. Of course the Department of Child Services, and the adoption agency looked into Mr. Zimmerman's home situation. There was no legal reason to remove little Robert from the home, and there certainly was no law against a single man raising his own adopted child. Still, we could tell he wasn't comfortable with the responsibility of caring for the boy alone. His sister agreed to stay on for a few weeks. During that time, having family around was a big help. When it was time for her to leave, Mrs. Lillian Lapp popped in whenever she could, bringing extra meals, and helping with some of the household duties. After a bit, she arranged for her daughter, Nellie to help out. It was no secret that Mr. Zimmerman was now a widower with a young child to attend to, and some folk who had available daughters were afraid that Mrs. Lapp was planning to fix up a right nice situation for her own daughter. Of course that was silly talk, because we all knew that Nellie was too young for marriage. She still had one more year to go in school, and one could expect that the last thing on her mind was trying to be tied down to an older man, and his son. After all, she was probably just starting in her *'Rumschpringe'*.

Nellie only came to watch the toddler while Mr. Zimmerman worked out in his shed, supposedly making some kind of headway on what he did to earn a living, but she was sure that most of his time was spent just sitting there in his grief. She was only allowed to stay during the day, and left after she prepared the noonday meal. I met her a few times on the road, just to ask how things were going for him. From what I could understand, Mr. Zimmerman was in sort of a dilemma. It was dreadfully hard on him in the evenings she said. It wasn't because of the cooking, or having to do meals, most of the People took care of that; especially neighborly ladies with marrying age, or *Maidel* daughters. Most women in general were very respectful of a persons time in their grieving, but some on the other hand could be kind of forward.

It could be very difficult on anyone trying to explain to a toddler why his Mamm wasn't coming home any more. Mr. Zimmerman, as with most men, was not one to openly share his feelings with a woman. Nellie could only guess that his nights were long and tiresome, because of the way he looked in the mornings. He was ruffled, and had dark circles under his eyes. She was just a teenager, but she was concerned about what would happen to them when she went back to school in September. Who would be there for the little toddler? I told her, those were questions that only the Heavenly Father knew how to answer, and we would just have to wait and see what the outcome would be.

chapter

TWO

Somehow, my thoughts kept turning to Laverna Zimmerman. They weren't exactly thoughts of grief, although I was very much grieved, but almost as if I knew she wanted me to help her husband in some way. I shared these feeling with Mamm. But, as usual, she was not hasty to give answers to questions better left to the Lord. I didn't know what to think of these feelings. I would have liked to help, but I could not break the law. I had to keep to the adoption agreement. Even if I could help, I didn't want my caring and personal attention for Robert Jr. to be mis-understood by Mr. Zimmerman for something more than what it was. I knew within my heart of hearts that one day my beloved would return to me, and that is all I hoped for. In the Amish community, the People were quick to play matchmaker, and things are hard enough as it is. A little too much interest in a certain way could set the tongues a wagging, and well…I surely didn't need that added attention.

I thought, *'What if Mr. Zimmerman should decide to go back home to his family, and take my son across state lines?* He could, because Robert Jr. is his legal adopted child; what's to prevent it? He can move anywhere he wants to. The thought of such a thing sent me in a frenzy. I knew I could never bear it. I prayed so much that week; I did all I could do to keep my imagination from running away with me, and also from running up the road to beg for my child. Nellie told me Mr. Zimmerman was not doing well, and it only made me want to be by my child's side all the more. Encountering certain pressures and stress can make people do strange things they wouldn't ordinarily do; like becoming *'verhuddelt'* – confused, or make spur of the moment decisions. Who knows that better than me?

～～

On one of my better days, I got the courage to want to do something about my fears. Just about the time I was going to leave the house to walk up to the shanty to call for a taxi, I met Mrs. Miller headed towards our home. I got so nervous thinking that she was on her way to the house to bring good news about Robert that I got weak in the knees. The news wasn't what I had wished it to be, but it was for me. My intent was to get in touch with Mrs. Bell to see if she could share with me anything that would help me to know what kind of plans Zack was making concerning Robert Jr. The news from Mrs. Miller was, that Mr. Zimmerman wanted to meet with me the very next morning. She said it had already been cleared with Child Services. I had no idea what was on his mind, and didn't know if whatever he had to say would be good news, or bad. Before I left the house, I asked Daed and Mamm to pray with me.

The temperature was already on the rise by 9:00am. I had hoped that wasn't a sign of what was to come. Ordinarily, on a late August morn like this, I would have been in my bare feet, but thinking a little more maturely now, I knew that was no way to visit a widower's home. I had begun to dress more Mennonite, than Amish, so I put on a fresh, crisp, white apron over a light blue dress that had very thin white line in the fabric. I still had my hair pulled back in a tight bun roll at the back of my neck, and I allowed my 'kapp' strings to hang gently down the front of my shoulders. Sometimes in these past days, I wore my hair in a ponytail fastened with a barrette, but that was mainly for around the house. I gave myself a good twenty-five minutes for the fifteen-minute walk. I was a little 'naerfich'-nervous when I set out, but a few prayers along the way helped to settle my stomach. I took my time, and rejoiced in God's presence. I knew I wouldn't be late. I just didn't want to have beads of sweat on my forehead when I arrived. I came around the clump of trees near the road, and turned to face the drive that lead up to Zechariah Zimmerman's house. I froze in my tracks when I saw two *Englischer's* vehicles parked in the front yard. "**Ach**, What the world!"

That day changed my entire life, and set me in a whirlwind. I just knew in my heart that I had lost my sweet, precious son forever. There's nothing I could have thought, or even could have imagined that would come close to making sense of the next hour that was at hand.

I whispered another prayer for strength, and for God's will to be done, then forged ahead. I went to the back door (as is our custom), and gave a light tap on the side wood panel of the screen. Mr. Zimmerman appeared a few seconds later. He bade me *"Guder mariye"* (Good morning), then stepped back from the door so I could enter. I couldn't quite read the expression on his face. Was it disappointment, fear, or just plain nerves? Even though they had been our neighbors, I had not had much personal contact with them, especially with Mr. Zimmerman. He set out leading the way through the kitchen to the living room area. All of a sudden it hit me. *I'm going to see my son. I'm going to see my own little boy, up close.* My mind, and emotions ran amuck. I began to feel faint, and had to steady my steps as I entered the room. The visitors were sitting on the Settee. I immediately recognized the Negro woman. It was Mrs. Bell, the lady from Child Services. *How odd,* I thought; the very one I wanted to call on yesterday. She's the one who helped to place my twins. The other woman holding Robert Jr. was occupying his attention with her set of car keys. Both of the women greeted me, and Mr. Zimmerman offered me a seat. I sort of dropped in the one closest to where I was standing. It was the cane-back chair near the entrance to the room. I was truly befuddled, even to the point of tears, although I don't know why. This was the closest I had been to my baby boy in nearly three years. I felt the blood drain from my head. My eyes became bleary, and the last thing I remembered was my body slowly slipping from the chair to the floor.

~~

Officer Bill had been with the police department for almost ten years. Something in him never healed, and was still a hurting twinge in his conscience because of the way he just upped and left his family one day; leaving his boy with relatives. The one thing that tore at him most was the way he never stayed in touch with him. Now, walking in his newfound faith, he knew he had to right several wrongs, starting with himself. Since that incredible encounter at the train depot a few years ago, there had been no more news about the missing soldier, Robert. Bill felt lead to start out on his own in search for his son. Ten years on the force wasn't a long time, but it did allow for a small pension, and he had also saved some extra money in a retirement fund. He hung around Lancaster for about six more months; because he still had a few lose ends to tie up there concerning his personal life. He wanted to check into what he should do about the alias name *Robert Williams* he currently went by. After all, he was born Johnathan Holfman. One decision he made was to take his pension retirement in a one-lump sum package. That way, he wouldn't have to receive mail every month at any particular address under his name, or any other name should that be the case. To help reestablish his past identity, he thought he could open a bank account in the name of Johnathan Holfman. But, that would not work, at least not for now because the bank would need a current ID, and address to establish his account, and he didn't have that either.

Bill thought back to how he first got into this situation. He was shunned, in a round about way from returning back to his father's place. As a young man ready to take over the family orchard, he thought the illegal *booze* racket was a good way to get rich quick. Instead, it landed him in jail. Prohibition was over, but making illegal whiskey was still a crime. After serving his three-year sentence, there was nowhere for him to go when he was released. He couldn't go back to Walnut Creek. By that time, his sister Rebecca had married an English guy, and they moved back East. Because, William, his younger brother was killed being robbed at gunpoint, that left his folks all alone, except for Mr. Miller, and his family who live in the small sharecropper's house on the east end of the property. He surmised because of their apparent situation, not having any more children at home that could help with the orchard, they must have asked the Millers to move from the sharecropper's dwelling to the main house. The Millers had always helped with the farm, and the orchard, but his family would have been too large to move in the *Dawdi Haus*, (usually set aside for the elderly, or for grandparents). Bill thought of the times he had to come back to Walnut Creek, but he didn't chance on going up on the property. It was easy to get Amish news. A short drive down Old Philadelphia Pike, Interstate 340 would land him in *Bird-in-Hand,* and a few miles down from there, was the town of *Intercourse.* Over the years he subscribed to either the "The Circuit", or "the Budget" the Amish newspapers. Aside from that, he also had an inside source who kept him abreast on what was happening with his family. Because of that source, he was able to come back for his Mamm's, and his Daed's funerals. He viewed them from a distance, but at least he had the peace of being there.

Bill got up from his easy chair, went to the bathroom and viewed his image in the mirror once more. He knew from his first experience a couple of year's back, not to show up near Strasburg with a clean-shaven face. During the six months following his retirement, he grew a thin mustache, and now, sported a close fitting beard; nothing outlandish like the 'Old-Order Amish', but neat and trim, close to the face. It looked all right, but felt a little strange to him, because he had always been a clean-shaven type of guy. Some of this had to do with his job as a police officer, but mainly because that's the way he liked it. However, because his last trip to Strasburg caused a couple of eyebrows to rise, he figured that he and Robert must have favored more than he thought they would, and he found that to be true from their first accidental meeting several years back. The truth of the matter is, he thought, *'I'm living the life of a person who doesn't really exist, and it has affected more lives than just mine. But, what could I do back then? I was twenty-two years old, and couldn't keep a job once they found out about my record'.* At that time he remembered thinking; *the next time I land a job, I'll give then a different name.* And that's exactly what he did. When filling out the form for the boarding house, he wrote down the name...Robert, Robert Williams. It wasn't altogether a strange name to him. His brother's name was *William*. So, when he found a place looking for part-time help; he wrote Robert Williams on the application. Most of the workers started calling him Bill. He wasn't quite sure if it was an English thing, or if they did it to distinguish between he and the other William at the plant.

During the last few months, Bill tied up as many loose ends as possible. He closed out all of his accounts, and as far as the few friends he had; he told them he was headed to Ohio to rejoin his long lost family. Although, he was the one who was long lost. He wasn't too concerned about them looking him up. They were more of acquaintances, than friends. He still was not sure how he was going to handle the situation of his name change. *Maybe,* he thought, *I'll look up a lawyer, or some attorney when I get relocated near Brewster, and see what can be done. Starts County seemed like a good place to live, but I'm sure that won't be my final destination. It's close enough to Strasburg, and Walnut Creek without...well, without chancing upon old acquaintances.*

Rachel's news of being summoned by Zachariah raised concern in Anna Zook's spirit, but she did not want to worry about it. Yet, she still wondered, *Ach, why does he want to see my Rachel?* She knew better than to stir up questions in her mind. It was already bad enough that the 'grapevine' of idle gossip was in full swing. It was already pairing off Rachel with Zachariah to be matched up soon; even though she had kept her distance from his home, and he had not come to visit their home, *even once,* since his wife Laverna passed away. Ordinarily, this could have been an ideal situation, a young *'Maidel' (a woman who has never been married),* and a widower. Except, for a few details that the People weren't aware of. One, Rachel was not a 'Maidel'. She surely believed with all her heart that her husband was still alive. And two, not only was she not a single woman, but she was also a Mamm (Mother). The People may not have known this, but Mr. Zimmerman did. Anna Zook thought aloud, "Ach, …now what the world can be going on in that young man's mind?" One thing she knew, 'for sure and for certain'; *The good Lord heavenly Father would not disappoint.*

༄

Rachel could feel a cool towel across her forehead. Mrs. Bell was standing at her side holding her hand.

"Rachel, my dear. Are you all right? No don't try to get up."

"What's going on, what happened"?

Mr. Zimmerman chimed in, "You must have fainted. Maybe it was the shock of being in the same room with you son."

He was right. I longed to hold my baby for so many years, I guess the experience of being this close to him, was overwhelming.

Once it was established that I was not really ill, they proceeded. The news that followed almost caused me to faint again. It brought tears to my eyes, and an ache in my heart. *What?* I could not believe my ears. I was to have my child back. *Nee-* no, this can't be possible. What miracle has God wrought?

Mr. Zimmerman had decided he would put the farm up for sale, and move back to Pennsylvania with his family. He explained to the social workers that staying here, and trying to raise Robert Jr. without his wife brought on even more grief for him, knowing a child was the very thing his wife wanted so much. Evidently, while the agency looked in on the Zimmerman's, they were also secretly checking up on me. They were astonished to find that I was keeping my promise not to visit, or to interfere with the Zimmerman's raising of my child. When Zachariah first met with them, more than two months before this day, it was upon his suggestion, and request that Robert be returned to his natural mother. He knew his wife would have wanted it that way. After all, the babies were only put up for adoption because of my youth, and my religion. Neither one of those was a factor now. Instead of being seventeen, I was nearly twenty, and had proven her maturity in more ways than just my age.

Since Nellie Lapp would be returning to school, Rachel could begin having small visits, taking care of light household chores, and helping with her *own* beloved baby boy. The visits would be semi-regulated until all the proper paperwork was completed, and then it would be up to Mr. Zimmerman and me how the transition would occur. But, for as much as I could understand, within the next thirty days I would be officially deemed the legal parent and guardian of Robert Jr. The agency would also take care of making any changes needed on the birth certificate, although Robert was already listed as the legal father of the twins...*um, the twins.*

Walking back down the road toward home seemed like a never-ending journey, but Rachel was sure it couldn't have taken more than the ten to fifteen minutes it took to walk up that road less than one hour before.

chapter

THREE

Rachel's visit to Mr. Zimmerman's house was the most incredible experience her parent's had ever heard. Yet, they knew it was because the hand of God was at work. Though only a few people knew of Rachel's situation, those few believed with her for her answered prayers. Rachel and her parents clearly understood that the present rejoicing brought remembrances of an ever-constant void; not just the void of her 'Lizzy', but also of her beloved husband... Robert. Anna Zook encouraged her daughter by letting her know she believed when God answers your prayer, He answers the whole prayer. Because God knows you on the inside, He remembers the prayers that stay upon your lips, as well as the prayers that stay upon your heart. He is sovereign, and knows how much we can bear. She told her daughter that God knows the good, and the bad of bearing sorrows. Sometimes we don't think we can bear the bad, but if we trust Him... we can. She wanted Rachel to understand that God can send answers to prayers in increments, a little at a time, until the whole prayer is answered. She knew that quite well, because He did it for her.

Rachel thought how difficult this must be for Mr. Zimmerman. Moving away would solve some of his problems, but maybe it wouldn't solve all of them. She prayed that his sorrow would not be added to. Rachel knew how much he loved little Robert, as if he was his own. She could only imagine how hard it must be to carry mixed emotions of love about someone in your heart. But, *Who would know that better than me,* she thought? How many times, when he's gone, will he want to reach out and hold Robert Jr. in his arms, but the comfort he'll get from memories, will constantly remind him of what he has lost. Poor Zack. He had the legal right to take his son with him, but still, that would not lessen his grief for Laverna? He was a man torn between two loves, and surly needed our prayers. It must have been torment to hear Robert Jr. ask, "When is Mamm coming home?" How can one explain that to a little child? *Ach, Rachel thought, I guess I'll be in Mr. Zimmerman's shoes pretty soon, and I'll be needing the same prayer to cover me.*

⁓

Elizabeth stopped in to visit her parents while Ben made a few deliveries. His wood working business had picked up last year, especially since he consigned some of his handiwork out to Jonas Yoder's store. Ben met Jonas a few years back when he was looking for a place to live. In fixing up the house where we were going to live, he stopped in the hardware store a few times to get things he needed. On one occasion Mr. Yoder said Ben could have some tools from his shop. They reached an agreement for him to pay off the tools a little at a time, until the balance was down to zero. Ordinarily, that would not have been the way Ben handled finances, but he was building a corner shelf for my wedding day surprise, and he just didn't have the extra money at the time to invest in a set of carving tools. Other than stopping in the hardware store for little things like nails, sandpaper, and varnish, Mr. Yoder had no real reason to trust Benjamin with his tools, except for the fact that they must have taken an immediate liking to each other. Besides, he was mighty curious to see the finished product.

When Ben was finished with the cabinet, he invited Mr. Yoder to come out and see the finished corner shelf. While he was there he helped Ben move it inside to the kitchen. He brought his wife, April alone with him. She looked around the house, and said Ben had made a fine choice, that any woman would be proud to have such a nice home like this. Ben said it was April Yoder who ask if she could come back later with her sister, and help redd-up (clean up) the place, and not to worry, they had plenty of cleaning supplies. He offered to pay them for their help, but they refused, saying it was their wedding gift for his new 'fraa'-wife. It was Mrs. Yoder and her sister who said they knew where he could purchase a small, used refrigerator that would be just perfect for the kitchen. With all the help he got from people he hardly knew; it made him look prêt good in my eyes on our wedding night to move in a house already made into a home.

Elizabeth cried tears of joy when she heard the news about Rachel. She loved her sister dearly, and ached for her happiness. It was a difficult thing to watch someone so full of loving kindness, be in such turmoil these past few years. Being so happy myself, caused me at times, to feel a little guilty about Rachel. I never minded the extra time Rachel spent holding Abraham when he was just a wee one. I watched Rachel carefully when it was time for visits to be over. She would hug him a little tighter, and cuddle him a little bit longer, but I never once suggested that Rachel might be getting too attached to her nephew...at least not out loud. I didn't have to, because it seems that Rachel would sense it in her spirit, and put restraints on her actions.

The same afternoon Rachel received the news; Anna Zook had a chance to talk with both of her daughters. There would be many things to consider, and many more that would need God's providential wisdom. She didn't want the situation to appear bleak, but first, Rachel had to consider her secret marriage, and her expecting her wee ones was only known by four families in the district: the Zook's, Ben and Elizabeth, the Millers, the bishop and Aendi (Aunt) Mae Zook. The question of why Mr. Zimmerman would allow his adopted son to be left in the care of Rachel, when there were so many available Amish families in the district that could take him, was sure to come up. Then the tongue waggers would try and draw their own conclusion, which would probably be all wrong. It also would place bishop Daniel in an awkward position to answer the inquiry of why he would allow an Amish baby (as far as they knew) to be brought up in the house of a family who had been 'shunned'. Mamm didn't mention all of these things to Rachel, for surly she had enough to pray about, but she could see that, what was once a family secret would eventually become a very public matter.

≈

Mr. and Mrs. McAfee paced the emergency room corridor of Lancaster General Hospital. Mr. McAfee didn't usually drive, but Jacob was in such terrible pain that afternoon when he drove back from working on the little house over in Hempfield Township, they thought he should go to the hospital. Evidently he was in the process of renovating some of the rooms inside. He thought if the place was fixed up, maybe they could rent it out for the extra money they needed to help subsidize Mr. McAfee's retirement check, or maybe they could put it up for sale. Jacob wasn't sure that they were too interested in owning rental property because of the work it took for upkeep. Jacob knew that his spirit had become a little restless. He wasn't sure why, but he was sure that the dreams he had been having had something to do with his feelings. He loved the elderly couple, but hanging around being the caretaker for the community was not in his final plans. Daniel and Dessie Rea McAfee were like parents to him; yet he knew within him that it would soon be time for him to move on.

He was painting the ceiling in one of the small bedrooms when he seemed to have painted himself out of that area of the ceiling. Rather than to take the time to climb down from the ladder, and move it to where it would be more accessible, he decided to dip the roller in the paint pan once more, and reach for the spot in back of him. Needless to say, he lost his grip; fell sideways from the ladder, hit his head against the radiator on his way to the floor, and landed on his shoulder. As it was, because of his medical condition, he really did not want to go to a hospital. He decided a few months ago he could no longer wait for his real identity to come back to him; and the only thing to do was to get out there and find it. He didn't like breaking the law, and he loved the Mr. and Mrs. McAfee too much to take a chance on getting them in trouble, and driving their car without a proper driver's license was one of those reasons. Most of his time was spent helping the McAfee's, and he didn't know what they would do without him, but Daniel was the one who encouraged him to venture out, saying, *every man needs to have a little money of his own in his pockets.* It all worked out fine. That is, until he knew he needed something more. He really wanted to find out who he was. For all he knew, he was a married man, and maybe he was even a father. Although, he answered to the name Jacob, he was only sure of two things; he was wearing a wedding band, and the name Rachel was inscribed inside it. *That must be the girl that visits me in my dreams. Strange he thought...I could never clearly see her face.*

One of the attending nurses came out to let Daniel, and Dessie Rea know that the doctor would be admitting

Jacob. The examination showed that he had a small frac-
tured of the shoulder bone, and the knot on his head from
the fall, had some swelling. They had already placed him
in his room, planning to keep him for observation and
x-rays. The nurse guided them to the elevator closest to
the nurse's station on his particular floor. From there they
could be directed to Jacob's room. When they arrived, Dr.
Al Westly was still with his patient. He was reviewing
the clipboard he held in his hand, and giving the nurse
instructions for pain medication. They waited quietly at
the door, not knowing if to enter the room, or not. The
doctor put the clipboard under his arm, and waved them
into the room. Dessie Rea spoke first.

"Well, doctor, how is he?"

"Oh, I think he'll be okay. We're giving him something for the pain. It'll help him to rest too."

He allowed them to speak to Jacob for a little bit,
before motioning them to follow him out. He said they
could return in a few minutes, that he would probably
still be wake. While they completed some admitting
forms, he wanted to know if there was anything else he
should know about his patient that would help with his
speedy recovery. The couple informed him that Jacob was
not there son. When they explained how he came to stay
with them, and the present condition he was in, Dr. Al
was grateful for the information. It was something to be
added to his chart. The McAfee's wanted to stay through
the night, but Dr. Westly convinced them to go home
and get a good night's sleep. It was the best thing they
could do for now. Daniel gave Dr. Westly the name, and
phone number of the physician who had seen Jacob when

they first found him. They left the hospital feeling a little more confident, knowing that Jacob's room was only two doors down from the nurse's station, and if there were any change, they would give them a call. Meanwhile, Dr. Al thought he would make a few telephone calls.

Jacob woke from his dream. He knew he was dreaming because it was the same one he had several times before. But, as most dreams go, every time he dreamt it, it was a little different. He could never put a whole scene together well enough to tell someone about the dream, and it not sounding crazy. In his dream he was always looking in on it, like he was viewing a movie, or something, except sometimes he knew the main character was himself. The girl kept changing, not all together, but in the way she appeared. Sometimes she was a pretty light skinned Negro girl, maybe in her late teens, and other times she was the half modern, half *schoolmarm* looking type of girl, sort of straight laced. She wasn't ugly, just a little plain. From the inscription in his ring, his guess was that the girl in his dream was this Rachel. But, *Who was she?* Which girl was she?

It seemed that neither one of the girls lived in the inner city. They were always walking down a country road, or standing at one of those roadside fruit stands. Sometimes she was coming out of a barn that had big double doors. At times, she would turn around to catch him looking at her, and would just smile, or give a friendly wave. In his dream he'd try to read what her lips were saying, but could not make it out. *Strange, he thought; the way he could see her smile, and her lips, but could not see her face clearly.* Other people passed in, and out the dream.

He could even hear background noises, and them calling him, or saying his name, but he could never remember what the name was.

He must have been squirming around in his bed in an attempt to wake from his dream, because when he opened his eyes, the night attendant was standing at his bedside checking his I V.

"How are we doing", she asked, still going about her work, *not really expecting an answer.*

"Ya must have been in a little discomfort. You were moving around a bit. But, we didn't want to administer any pain medication, until we hear from the patient how he's feeling".

She was a middle-aged woman, a little on the plump side. She was very pleasant, and something seemed so familiar about her voice.

"Now, young man", she said, "I'm going to lift your head a bit to check on the lump you put on the back of your noggin. Umm, t'is still there, but the swelling's gone down some. There's just a *wee* bit of a bump now, so we still have to be careful. Do ya need anything?"

"Well", I managed to say. "If it's not too much trouble, I'd like a little something to take the hunger off my stomach."

She went around to the end of the bed, removed the clipboard from the hook, and read down through the chart.

"Well, I don't see anything here that says ya can't have something to eat. Looks like you slept through the supper hour. For some reason it's been a busy night around here. I'll go and make my report, and then I'll have a *look-see* to see what I can find."

She was about to leave the room, but turned back to come and tuck the blankets back in around his legs, and see that the railing was secure. As she was leaving the room, she said:

"Ach, for pity sakes, it seems like the hurrier I go, the behinder I get."

At that last statement something clicked in Jacob's mind.

chapter

FOUR

Rachel tried to have faith in the prayers she prayed, but it seemed to be of little use. The stress of carrying such a burden was almost too much to bear. How much did God expect a nineteen-year-old girl to handle? After thinking what she thought, Rachel had to repent, and ask for forgiveness; admitting to herself...*after all, you did have something to do with how this situation began.* She felt so guilty taking a man's child away from him... because that's really how she felt. But, why did she feel that way? There was nothing to feel guilty about. This child was hers. Zachariah even told her she had nothing to feel guilty about, because he and the good Lord made this decision together, just like the decision was made earlier when Robert Jr. first came to them. He said he finally realized that adopting a child was much more for his wife's benefit than his own. It wasn't that he didn't want a child, but maybe this was the way the Lord was answering his wife's heart's desire. Laverna had so many discouragements in her life; the way Zack looked at it, was that God lent to her a little happiness before he called her home, and He allowed Rachel to be a part of it. He said he always wanted children, and even when they went to visit a doctor before moving to Walnut Creek, the doctor said just for the fact that his wife could get pregnant proved that the problem did not rest with him. She was just unable to carry a baby full term. Zack said, Laverna would often apologize to him for being such a failure as a wife, but he never thought that of her. He loved his wife more than anything. He said he always believed that when her illness improved, they would be able to have a child; still she kept trying, even in her frail state of health.

Jah, Rachel thought, it was a terribly hard thing for Mr. Zimmerman to explain to Robert Jr. why his Mamm was never coming home again, but it was going to be even harder on her explaining to him why the only Daed he ever knew wasn't coming back either.

The plan was to have Rachel come to the house to cook, and to look after the household as much as possible. That was for the first week. She was to leave sometime after the noonday meal was prepared. That way she would have spent enough time with Robert Jr., and could go back to check on things at the house to see if she was needed there. When she returned, she'd put the toddler down for his nap, so she could redd-up the house for their evening meal. On Mondays, she came early in the morning to do the laundry. Mondays were washday in the Amish community. When Robert Junior... *hum;* she thought, *I think I'd like to have a nick name to call him once he's fully mine.* The Zimmerman's just called him Robert, which was not a name usually given to an Amish boy, but she was appreciative that her request had been honored as part of the adoption appeal. *When his Daed returns, we can't call both of them Robert, now can we? It was kind of odd that such a thing should pop into her head.*

Rachel never gave up true hope that one day her forbidden love would return to her. It was just at that instant that the thought of him being a *Dad* came so naturally. After she prepared the evening meal she woke Robert Jr., and brought him down to the kitchen for his snack. She pushed the wooden highchair up close to the table to make sure his diced foods were reachable. Actually, he did pretty good eating with a spoon, although sometimes he would have an *oopsy* or two. Like with most toddlers, the fork was a little more challenging. No matter! Rachel was always prepared with a towel tied around his shoulders like a bib, and another one on the floor to catch any fragments of food that escaped. A few of these little tricks she learned from babysitting her own 'kinder' siblings. Mamm suggested for her to bring the young'n over to the house a few mornings starting the following week. It would give him a chance to experience another environment; to see other people's faces that had visited his own home, and also for Rachel to judge where his trust level with her was beginning to lie. Would he turn to her, or search her out when she was out of his sight for more than a few minutes? How was he with strangers? Had he began to adapt to her voice, her care...her love?

⌒⌒

Bishop Daniel Zook paced the bedroom floor several times. When he'd finish pacing the short distance from the bed to the door, he'd stand still for a moments, shake his bearded chin a few times, then make an about-face, and walk back to the bed again.

"I just don't understand it", he said aloud. "Why is it that Abraham Zook's family gives me more trouble than the Lord allows, and I do mean than the *good* Lord allows! At least, I try to think that it's not Him who is allowing it."

Mae Zook knew her husband well enough to know that these questions were rhetorical, and were meant *not* to answer. To interrupt his thinking aloud with an answer he did not want to hear would not only, *not* help the present situation, but further aggravate it, so she remained silent.

"I'm prêt near sure no other bishop in the whole district, **Nee**; the whole region, has to go through these kinds of decisions that I've had to make, especially when it comes to *that* family."

Well, she knew his dandruff was raised now by the way he referred to his brother's family as *'that'* family. The best thing for her to do at the moment was to say a silent prayer. First, she would pray that her bishop-husband would not be weakened to sin during his present storm of agitation. Then, she would pray for his spirit to calm down enough so he could actually hear from the Lord; that is if the good Lord heavenly Father was saying anything to him at all. It must be frustrating not to have a past case, or another incident that was similar to this one to reflect on, or at least to compare it to. Bishop Zook continued to talk.

"I've always tried to uphold my appointment as bishop with integrity, and honor. So, why am I always being tested like this?"

"I'm sure I can't say dear." Mae felt this was a safe response.

"You would think that with all the leniency I have shown Abraham, and *his* family, they would try to make my standing in the community a little more pleasant."

"Daniel, I know how you must feel, but try to remember that none of these incidences were of his choosing either."

She almost said, except for him choosing to follow Christ; but caught herself in time. And almost as if he had read her mind, he retorted:

"Jah, but he did choose to deny his faithful commitment to the church, and become *saved,* now didn't he?"

Mae remained silent. She knew how hurtful it must have been for her husband to go through these trials. Not only did he have to issue the *'Bann'* on his own brother and his wife, but that he himself was called before the bishops. At this point, he wasn't sure if his standing as bishop was jeopardized because of his inability to dissuade his family members from abandoning their allegiance to the Amish church, but he could sure feel that eyes were on his every move. That's one of the reasons he was so worried by Mae's visits to Jesse's and Mary's house. Some visits to her Mennonite family had always been tolerated; but now, it was the ones he knew Mary had secretly arranged for Anna to be in on that made him uneasy. He couldn't blame her much. Daniel Zook understood how difficult it was to have family members shunned; after all, his brother whom he was very close to, could no longer visit, or have any communication with him.

He missed the company of their fellowship very much. They couldn't attend Sunday meetings, Amish gatherings, or even weddings and funerals. The People were to shun them in public places. If they happened to show up in the same place at the same time, they were supposed to turn their backs on them, or leave out and come back later to transact their own affairs. The bann was a harsh thing. It affected more than the immediate family, it affected the whole Amish community, but it was put in place as a tool to help those who strayed away to see the error of their ways, and hopefully return to the faith.

Daniel was not a young man, and his wife could see how this shunning had taken a toll on his spirit, and his body too. The People looked to him, as bishop, for answers in their time of need. She didn't know how the good Lord would accept what she was thinking, *but how could the servant who was appointed to advise and care for others, help them, when he needed help himself?* He sometimes use to discuss things with his brother, deacon Abraham, but who could he turn to now...*just the good Lord I 'spose*, she thought. He could always discuss situations with her; some husbands and wives relationships were just that close, however, she respected the unspoken rule that a woman was not to meddle in her husband's affairs. She would wait until she was asked. Still, she wondered if there were other male relatives, or friends he could confide in. There was Jesse, but he was strictly Mennonite, or maybe he could talk thing over with preacher Beiler, but he was a pastor under her husband's *own* tutelage for pity-sakes. How could he confide in him? She didn't know what to do, or even if to do anything at all, so she just prayed for God's infinite wisdom in the matter.

〜〜

By week three of the decision, Rachel had completed all paperwork required of her, except for one little thing she wanted to be settled. Only a small group of people knew of her marriage. It was now time to set the record straight, and reveal her secret marriage to Robert Williams. This little piece of information may be the very evidence that would help the children in the future; although she was not sure how. She knew she felt strongly about getting it down somewhere in *black* and *white*. The Child Welfare Agency knew that the children were hers, which was a matter of record; besides, they were there when she delivered them. What they did not know was that Rachel was married at the time to the father of her twins. The agency suggested for her last name to be listed as the given name for the twins since they were going to be adopted at birth. The only thing they would allow to be on the birth certificate was the first name of the father. Only her parents, the Millers, and her sister and brother-in-law knew who the father was. The authorities reasoned, since each of the babies was to be adopted by different homes, they didn't think it advisable to have a father's last name on the certificates. Anyway, at the time, they were under the assumption that she had been a victim of foul play, and she did not know the father's last name. Rachel now wished she had thought things through a little better before she had agreed to their suggestions, but she was not aware of worldly laws, and her parents were just as perplexed as she was.

This latest news about her situation would be shared in a letter to bishop Daniel Zook. Most of this he already knew, but Abraham Zook thought it might be helpful in some way to his brother when the news about Rachel getting care of brother Zimmerman's child got out. This letter would give the bishop permission to release Rachel's story.

chapter

FIVE

When officer Bill arrived in Strasburg, he got a motel room, one of those that rent by the week, or the month. He had basically three things in mind; one to get a place to stay, two, to place his retirement money in a bank account, and three to find a job. It had been every bit of two weeks, and he had only accomplished two of the three things on his agenda. Because he had not yet resolved what to do about his given name, Johnathan Huffman, he still had some things to think through. Maybe that's why he was slow about finding work. This was bothering him to no end, and he had to do something about it. At any rate, once the legal stuff got cleared up, he could scout around for a place of his own to live. Staying in this motel was all right for a while, but he didn't want the expense of it eating away at his finances.

Bill wanted something to do to keep busy, but he didn't want to work hard. After all, he had put in his years with the police force up in Lancaster, and though retirement was nice, it wouldn't pay for him to become too lazy. He got a paper from up at the front office, and searched through the help wanted section. He circled a few things, but nothing really jumped out at him. There was another thing he kept in the back of his mind, and that was that he had to find work that wouldn't put him too close to family until he could feel good about what God's plan was, and what his next move should be. When his mind thought on it for a few minutes, he put the newspaper down, and went to the nightstand near the bed to get the telephone book.

Robert must have dozed off while his mind was thinking on what the night nurse said. *A lady's voice was calling to someone. The voice sounded distant, and a little distorted. Maybe I'm still dreaming he thought.*

"Hello there, I'm back with a little snack for you Jacob. I'll just raise your head up a bit, and swing the tray over the railing."

Wait a minute, he thought, clearing his head. She must be in the wrong room. But she can't be. I do remember asking about something to eat, but something must be mixed up...or is it me that's mixed up? My head might be a little woozy, but at least I ought to know my own name. The nurse was cheerfully going on about how she lucked into getting such a *'gut'* snack for him.

"Excuse me", he managed to say.

"Is there something else I can get for you Jacob?"

Robert blinked his eyes, and raised his right hand to his forehead.

"Excuse me", he said again, "but I think you have the wrong room, or maybe the wrong chart is on the bed. My name is not Jacob, it's Robert...*Robert Williams.*"

"What the world" she said aloud, and reached for the chart hooked at the end of the bed.

Giving it a quick look over she could see the name at the top read *Jacob McAfee.* Then, eyeing the next line, written in a bolder type were the words **Amnesia victim:** notify Dr. Westly if any unusual behavior, or changes take place. Not wanting to alarm her patient in any way, she said,

"Well, for pity sakes, of course, I'm so sorry. I'll just leave the tray here for ya, and see what can be done about this. No use wasting good food, that is if you're still hungry."

She tipped out of the room, and went immediately to the nurse's station to report the incident.

〰〰

Tina Marie was almost finished her last semester of college, and was still wondering what to do with her life. She constantly prayed over the past few years for the safe return of her cousin, and the caring mercy of God's grace to comfort her parents. Berlin Township wasn't too far from Walnut Creek, so she was able to come home most weekends if she wanted; weather permitting. Tina enjoyed her occasional visits with Rachel, especially when Rachel was living in her parents *Dawdi Haus.* It was private, and everything she needed was there; a kitchen, inside plumbing, a living room area downstairs, and a spacious bedroom upstairs along with a smaller room to be used for guest, or for storage if need be. When she was home for the summer, Tina spent a lot of time with her now, not so much Amish friend. Even though, technically they were related, calling someone your cousin-in-law was kind of silly, if not to say very complicated in their case. Besides, their relationship was more like that of sisters, than friends. After all, she was the one who kept Rachel's secret; that is, until it had to be revealed by Rachel.

Rachel and Tina stayed in touch through their letter writing. In her last letter to her sister-friend, Rachel told Tina Marie as much as she could about what was happening concerning Mr. Zimmerman's decision. On one of the trips into town Rachel rode with Mr. and Mrs. Miller to the adoption agency. They were to come along to verify the information about Robert being married to Rachel, and have it signed by a notary public. The fact that their nephew was still missing was an open womb every time they had to speak of him. Rachel knew how they felt. It was not an easy thing for them to do, but they had to sign papers deeming them as the legal grandparents of Robert Jr. since the whereabouts of the real father was unknown. Mr. and Mrs. Zook had to do the same paperwork, however, it was a little easier for them to handle.

⤜⤛

By week four, most of Robert junior's living conditions had maneuvered to the Zook's Dawdi Haus. Rachel decided she would give the nickname *'Bobby'* to her son. It was a bit *Americanized* for an Amish-Mennonite boy, but then again, his father was...*is* an American, and *very much an Englischer.* Her brother Jacob was about six years old now, but he would still enjoy having a younger sibling, of sort, to play with. It was unusual for the Amish to have such few children as Abraham and Anna Zook had, unless there was a real *gut* reason, and she knew it was, because a couple of years back, Mamm fell very ill with the beginning stages of Leukemia. That was when she and Daed's faith in the healing power of Jesus was strongly put to the test. Yes, because of the way Mamm was super naturally healed, I do believe in miracles. No, she won't be having any more children of her own, but she looks forward to a long life, and to all the *wee* ones Elizabeth and I will be having. Abraham (Abe) is Ben and Elizabeth's son, and is still a toddler. He's almost six months behind my Robert... *and my Lizzy.* Well, Jacob and *Bobby* may have a stretch of a few years between them, but they are warming up to each other as playmates. I think Jacob likes the idea of having someone around the house that is younger than he. On the other hand, my brother Moses, who is quickly approaching eleven, enjoys the idea of being old enough to be called *uncle.* It may just be my imagination, but I do believe his chest pokes out a little more when he's around Robert Jr.

❧

Zachariah Zimmerman sat in the cane-back armchair. With slumping shoulders, and his eyes tearful, he tried to work his way through this fog of loneliness. He didn't know how to handle his emotions. In the Amish culture he was taught to view death as God's choice, and *His* doing. For that reason, we are not to be given over to anger, or hard grieving for something that is God's Will. He could not stop the thoughts that ran through his head. *I feel guilty because I am hurting so much, but I can't let anyone know. Men aren't supposed to feel this way. That's what they tell me. Of course, we get a handshake, or a pat on the back from the brethren, and that is supposed to make everything okay. The women may be filled with compassion for you, because they know how you feel, but they politely offer their condolences, and move on.*

Some of Zachariah's grief came from self-pity, and his inability to handle simple things around the house. In growing up Amish, boys were taught nothing about inside housekeeping. They were taught to follow in their father's footsteps to do *'mans'* work. That could be why widowers remarry so quickly. He didn't know anything about cooking, or how to redd-up the house. If it had not been for the help of his neighbors, he would not have known some of the special care and attention that his own son needed. When he came in from the work shed, half the time he would wander around the house from room to room, or just sit in the cane-back chair gazing into nothingness.

Zachariah shook his head, trying to bring himself out of his stupor. He knew it would soon be time to make his way over to the Zook's for a visit. It was difficult for him to keep to his agreement of weaning his visit times down with Robert. The visits were to become fewer, and shorter as the next few weeks approached. It would be best for all concerned if they could begin to put a distance between them beginning now, rather than later. Hopefully, it would make it easier for the final parting. The neighboring ladies still saw to bringing meals for him. Sometimes they would bring the meal themselves, and at other times, they would send it by the men folk; that is if they were coming that way. It was good when the brethren came by. They were kind enough to say they didn't look at it as being errand boys for their wives, because they were eager for the chance to visit with me anyway. *Maybe this was alluding to the fact that I had withdrawn my attendance from most social gatherings, and even Sunday meetings.*

I enjoy Mrs. Miller's visits, and her cooking is something to be savored. I felt safe with her visits. Not only did she share, let's say some good *Motherly advice,* but, unlike some of the *maidels,* who were sent by their Mamms to bring meals, I didn't have to worry that I was expected to show her some special interest, just in case she was looking for a proposal of marriage.

It was good that Rachel now had charge of her son. One of the things I became aware of is that while he was here, I must have been unconsciously pouring my grief into him. I didn't mean to do it. I guess I was just looking for a way to comfort myself. I have another week, or so to go before my move back to Lancaster, Pennsylvania. My property is up for sale. The auction last week rendered a fare amount of cash, and Benjamin Esh said he and Mr. Yoder would bring the market wagon, or a truck over by next weekend to pick up the better things I sold to them. *It's strange how only a few years of someone's life can seem like a lifetime.*

chapter

SIX

When Johnathan Holfman randomly selected an attorney from the telephone book a few days back, he supposed things were going to be much more complicated than they turned out to be. Attorney Davis gave him some helpful suggestions as to what he could do about his unlawful use of his other name. He said that anyone could go to court and have his, or her name legally changed, as long as they had proof of their given birth name. They could petition the courts to keep the assumed name they (in this case, he) had been using, as long as he could prove he was not wanted for committing any crimes. Johnathan explained why the last thing mentioned might cause some problems, but attorney Davis didn't think so. The fact that he had once had a record might prove to be a proof positive for his identity; that is, because of his fingerprints. He said the rest of my information, paperwork, and blood test should be enough to attest to my true identity. Attorney Davis was sure that my excellent work record with the police department would work in my favor. I was glad I had stayed out of trouble, and had not worked under a different social security number, although I was concerned that I was using my assumed name when I got married. I was told not to worry about anything. The lawyer was sure that once my birth certificate checked out, and my other papers cleared, I would get positive results in a few days. Meanwhile, I went to find work as Robert 'Bill' Williams.

Bill wanted to work in the Strasburg area. He preferred to find some work near the downtown business community. Starks County was a pretty large place, and he still was not sure what he wanted to do. However, he was sure of two things, one, to stay away from the Strasburg Diner, and two, to stay away from Walnut Creek (at least for now). The last time he came that way, he drew suspicion to himself because of his slight resemblance to Robert. He hoped that with the thin mustache, and neatly trimmed beard he sported, this time he would be less recognizable.

Doctor Al had only gotten a few hours sleep when the phone rang at his house. Before he left to return to the hospital, he advised the nurse who called from the nurse's station to have a male staff attendant placed in the area, but not to enter the room until he arrived. Better to take precautionary measures, than to risk an unsafe situation later. One can never be too sure of how an amnesia patient will react when they are transitioning from their state of unconscious change, to present reality. It always helps, he thought, to have a familiar face, or family member around for them to relate to, but we may not have that advantage at this hour.

It was about 3:00am when Dr. Alvin arrived back at Lancaster General. The night nurse reported that Jacob, … or Robert had gone back to sleep. The pain medication was also an aid in that factor. He took the information from the nurse, and headed down to his office, leaving instructions to be notified as soon as the patient woke, but he hoped he would sleep through 'till morning; that way it would give him enough time to get the proper physicians in place to examine the patient for themselves. He would wait until morning before contacting Mr. and Mrs. McAfee. They were a little elderly, and already worried; he thought a good nights sleep would be in their best interest. Who knew what would occur in the morning? Would Robert know who they were, or would they be complete strangers to him?

⁓⁓

Abraham Zook was thankful the family agreed to give bishop Daniel permission to expose Rachel's story. Both Mary, and Mae told Anna that rumors were already circling in 'root' letters, and since, in most cases, one letter went from house to house, each household would add their own little bit of news; that is if it wasn't already mentioned. Though its primary use was to inform family of upcoming events such as weddings, expectant arrivals of 'wee' ones, and who was hosting the next *'Bee'*, it some-times got sidetracked into other things. Anna Zook knew the news about Rachel would spread like wildfire. She just hoped the rumors would get it right; that Rachel was married, *before* she was expecting her baby...*though not by much.* She was most thankful that the information released only mentioned one child. The bishop and Mae, the Millers, Mr. Zimmerman, and the agency were the only ones who knew of another child, a twin girl.

Rachel decided that with oncoming wagging tongues and curiosity seekers prying around, it may be best to stay close to the house. She could already detect gossip was aloft by the unusual amount of buggy traf-ficking on the main road just outside their turnoff lane. At least she felt safe inside her four walls. She was confi-dent her Daed would not allow any outsiders to approach the house, but than again, why would they? They didn't know anything about what was going on in the Amish community, and could probably care less. *There is nothing good about shunning* she thought, *but it has turned out to be a blessing in disguise. At least they didn't have to worry about the Amish community breaking the shunning restrictions.*

Rachel was concerned for Mr. Zimmerman. He had done nothing to be shunned for; so folk were apt to drop by his place unannounced for a *friendly* visit. *Ach, how dis-respectful can folk be?* She knew these last two weeks were a very hard thing for him to cope with. His visits were down to only two per week, and they were shorter each time. If anyone knew how hard it was to keep to agreements set by a legal contract, it was Rachel. She thought on Zachariah's last two visits. Robert Jr. was still comfortable with him however; she noticed that he kept tabs on her where a bouts too. She often thought of Zachariah's two loses, and grieved with him, even though some of the grieving was of her own. He wasn't a talkative man. But, he did share that he was thankful he had family to return to when he went back to Lancaster. He said he would stay with one of his brothers until he could readjust. He also received an invitation from someone on his wife's side of the family, but he said it seemed more of a formality, than a sincere offer. Somehow, in the back of his mind, he knew they had never forgiven him for moving Laverna away from her family in the first place. They never knew it was more of her idea to move than his, and he just never told them.

Zachariah wished the property would not take long to sell. He would only make a small profit off of his asking price, and he would use that to put in a trust fund for Rachel's twins. The money he got from the auction was for his traveling expenses, and what he needed to live on once he got back to his brother's. He knew his brother would not charge him anything for staying there, but he didn't want to appear to be a free loader just because he was grieving. He also wanted to put some aside for later when he looked for his own place. He just wasn't sure how the bishop in that district felt about bank accounts. He'd just have to wait and see. Zachariah had already spoken with Mr. Zook about the trust fund. He assured him arrangements could be made to open the account at the bank in Strasburg, and he could keep up the account in whatever way he wished.

Bill was in no way a mechanic, or the engineering type of guy, but when he saw the 'HELP WANTED' sign in the window of the hardware store, he went in to apply for the job. The shop was away from the direct downtown business area, sort of on the outskirts of town. He had done some tinkering around as a youth, and he *was* working as one of the custodians at the college when he met his wife. *Who knows*, he thought. I may not be "Mr. Fix-it", but I'm pretty sure I know enough to get by. Mr. Yoder said he could use an extra hand around the store, because of the way his furniture section was picking up. He didn't start out to carry any furniture, but because of Ben Esh, who had a special knack for unusual designs and special details in his wood pieces, some of his customers enjoyed coming in and selecting furniture ready made. That way, all they had to do was to select the color of stain they wanted, and have it varnished. His wife April, and his son Aaron helped with the business, but his wife's helping out made it hard for her to see to things at home like she wanted to. Aaron was not sure he wanted to stay and take over the family business; after all, there just wasn't much expansion to look forward to in the corner store hardware business. His idea was to get some extra learning on his own to help extend their business. He couldn't go to school, but his Daed would allow him to check out books from the library. He was drawn to some of the fancy furniture items made by Ben Esh. When he talked to his Daed about it, he said the city was growing, and they needed to grow with it. Even Mr. Yoder agreed to that.

While Bill was thinking about wanting to live a more relaxed style of life, now that he was retired, it seemed that Aaron Yoder was thinking the other way around. Change was out there, especially in America. On one of their occasions to deliver lumber and tools to a farmer's house, Aaron discussed some of his thoughts with Bill saying that, during the past years the youngest President in history (John F. Kennedy) had been elected to office; a black woman, Wilma Rudolph, won three Olympic gold medals, sex was being flaunted on the big screen in the person of Marilyn Monroe, and 250,000 people marched on the nation's capital for the cause of civil rights. It's not that America ought to stick her head in the sand like an Ostrich, but he felt it was high time that the *People* pulled theirs out. *It's kind of funny*, Bill thought to himself, *those are the very things that make me want to take a reprieve from the outside world. I feel it can only get worse, not better!*

Bill was pleased he had secured the job by the time Attorney Davis mailed him the letter for his court date. He was also a bit anxious, but he felt the favor of the Lord with him. There were a few things to be cleared up here and there, but for the most part it was now a matter of documentation, legally witnessing, and to notarize that Jonathan Holfman, born to Zeek and Hilda Holfman, and Robert J. Williams were one in the same person.

People had begun to call him 'Bill' as a nickname instead of 'Bob'. When he got out of prison, he kept the middle initial 'J' for Johnathan, but had chosen to use William for his last name. It was to honor his younger brother who was killed many years ago.

Bill left the courthouse that day feeling like a new man. There was a smile on his face, some pep in his step, and a weight lifted from his shoulders. Wow! How great is this he said to himself. I was able to keep my new name, and not lose my family birthright, should I ever need it to prove something in the future about my work history, and my pension. He was *gabedied (flabbergasted)!* He smiled at the Amish word that popped in his head.

Mixed emotions flooded Bill's heart. He wanted to celebrate, but on the other hand, he wanted to soak in the peace of all that just happened to him. He was too excited to be hungry, yet not quite calm enough to sit through a picture show. He certainly wasn't going to walk around town with a silly grin on his face, and he didn't want to go back to his rented room. He went to his car, and just sat there for a while. It was then that he realized he had no one to celebrate with, no one to share his joy, or accomplishments with. Bill started to feel a wave of melancholy come over him, and decided this was not the time to feel let down or depressed about anything. Snapping his fingers, and talking out loud he said, "That's it! I know just what to do." He remembered that little church Mr. Yoder told him about. It wasn't more than a couple of streets up past his motel. This is mid-week, he thought. They are bound to be having a mid-week service. It was already after four o'clock. This was one of the things he had neglected to do since his move. He would have just enough time to grab something to eat, shower, shave, and put on some of his good 'duds'. *Yes,* he smiled to himself, *I'll gather with the saint.*

chapter

SEVEN

Dr. Al Westly took the precautionary measures to order x-rays, and a CAT scan for his new patient. He sent paperwork down to Radiology to set Jacob's scans to begin at about 9:15am. If what the young man said was true, he needed to follow up with someone who was able to give him more information about Robert Williams. He called the nurses stations and gave a *'no food'* order, until after his test in the morning. It was still too early to notify Mr. and Mrs. McAfee about any changes, and anyway, he wanted to check with the Police Department, and the Bureau of Missing Persons to see if someone by that name, age, and description showed up in their records. If they couldn't give him any leads, maybe the McAfee's could. Still, he would try and use these few hours wisely.

❦

Donna loved her work at the hospital. She often thought of the sacrifice her parents made helping her to finish school, and allowing her to move back in with them as a single parent. Her previous office job was getting her nowhere. The pay was okay, but she wanted to do something more with her life than hold down a nine-to-five job. After the amazing goodness of God's grace in giving her 'Lizzy', she wanted to give back something to her fellow man. Living with her parents gave her the chance to finish studying for her nursing degree. The courses she had already completed, coupled with these additional ones, gave her what she needed to become an LPN. Now, she was the assistant nurse over Radiology.

When Donna Vaughn arrived at her station a little before 7:00am, she was filled in on the upcoming patient activity for the day. Radiology usually got an early start, and sure enough she was informed that Prep was scheduled for a new patient, Jacob McAfee, for x-rays, and a CAT scan. She had plenty of time to put staff in place for the 7:30a procedure. Anyway, she was sure the doctor would come down before too long to make certain everything was in order. Meanwhile, she asked the attendant at the station to stay alert for any buzzer signals coming from the room where the patient had been transferred.

❦

It seemed like the final days leading to Mr. Zimmerman's move rolled around quicker than Rachel had anticipated. She didn't know if she was ready for it.

In just a few more days she would be the sole parent of Robert Jr. By this time they had managed to refer to Mr. Zimmerman as *'Uncle Zack'*, which was comfortable for all involved. Bobby was already getting use to learning the name *'Gommy'* (grandmother) for Anna Zook. The word *'Grootmoeder'* (Dutch) for grandmother, was a little challenging for him to handle at the moment, besides, it was so formal. We had begun to refer to Mrs. Zimmerman as *'Aendi Mamm'*, an endearing term that would not disrespect the position Laverna held with Robert Jr. as his adopted mother, but also suggesting that this kind woman who was no longer in any of our lives had been sort of a caregiver Mamm. Bobby was just over two years old when Laverna died; one could not judge the impact a motherly presence has in a young child's mind. Another good thing to our favor, that is if you could call it good, was that the Amish did not take photographs, or keep pictures in albums; so there was no physical evidence that daily reminded the toddler of his early years with Laverna, …only the ones that may have been etched in his thoughts, by love.

※

This was the day Jonas Yoder was to go with his son Aaron to pick up the few remaining items from the Zimmerman place. Zack had some things for the hardware store, and the woodcarving tools Ben had brought at auction. April Yoder apologized over, and over again to her children.

"Ach, of all the days to be so *schlabbish*—careless. Not that any day is a good day mind ya."

She had been carrying several things, trying to avoid having to make two trips from the house to the barn, and slipped off the last step, and all because she had a piled up load in her arms. She fell, and twisted her ankle. Aaron, and Katie heard the commotion, and ran to her rescue. April was sure it was only a sprain, and assured the children she didn't need to be driven to town to see the doctor.

"For pity sakes", she scolded, 't'is just a little twist in the wrong way. If I can stay off my foot, I'll be just fine by tonight, or tomorrow morning."

April instructed Katie to get some ready-made ice cubes from the gas- powered refrigerator. She told her to wrap them in a clean kitchen towel, and crush the cubes with a hammer. Katie was full-grown, and knew well what to do, but just because she was back home living with her parents (after her failed marriage), Mamm at times, treated her like a young child. The failed marriage was not entirely her fault. Her husband Enos had run off with a *'fancy'* Englischer.

Aaron helped to get his Mamm back into the house, and over to the sitting room next to the kitchen. He got one of the low, four-legged stools they used to sit on for evening prayer, placed a cushion on it, and propped up her leg. After Katie came with the cold compress, she ran to put on the kettle to boil some water for tea. *Maybe a chamomile, or a ginger tea will help to calm Mamm's nerves; or maybe it was her nerves that needed to be calmed.*

Aaron could see the events of the day turning away from their original well-constructed plans. Mr. Yoder had already taken the open market wagon over to the store to get some canvas throws. He was going to wait until Aaron arrived before starting out for the Zimmerman place. If the weather held out, they would be fine. Originally, Mamm, and Bill Williams (the new guy) were supposed to watch the store while they were gone. Since Mrs. Beiler was probably headed their way about now, she was going to give Mamm a ride over to the hardware store, Aaron waited around to she if she could sit with her for a while, and he would have to go in to look after the store. Bill was a big help, but he wasn't experienced enough to handle regular customer, and the cash register. When Aaron got to the store, he filled his Daed in on everything that had happened at home, and assured Mr. Yoder that his wife was in good hands, and would be just fine. As a matter of fact, he said, when he left, it looked like Mamm was going to enjoy having company for the day.

〰

Dessie McAfee was up and stirring when the hospital rang their number. She was asked to hold for a call from Dr. Westly. Not knowing what was ahead, she called for her husband to pick up on the extension. The news brought on a mixture of emotions. She always prayed that one day, Jacob's memory would return, but was never quite sure how she would feel when it really happened. Now she knew. Dr. Westly explained that they were not certain how much memory was restored. He said by the time they got to the hospital, Jacob should be finished with the ordered examinations, and back in his new room. Daniel McAfee thought it wise to give themselves a little time to think before rushing out to the hospital, and since his wife had already started cooking breakfast, the best thing to do was to sit and have their meal.

Mrs. McAfee had come to love Jacob as she did her own departed son. She didn't want to be selfish. Both, she and her husband knew that it was only a matter of time before this passing stranger's memory would return to him, and he would be headed on his way. After all, he was probably somebody's husband, or fiancé, or even someone's father, although she thought him a bit young for that. Before they started out for the hospital, they joined hands and said a prayer, asking God's Will to be done. When Daniel went out ahead of Dessie to warm up the car, she slipped back to their room to retrieve the only other possession Jacob had with him that day, a small key that had the number *917* engraved on it. She put it in the outside pocket of her overcoat, and joined her husband in the car. The trip over to Lancaster General was more silent than none, but they didn't need words to know what each of them was feeling in their heart.

chapter

EIGHT

Nurse Vaughn prepped her patient for the upcoming procedures, and explained what was going to occur. Robert wished he could have been more helpful, but he didn't remember the answers to most of the medical questions he was being asked. He wasn't sure what medicines he was allergic to, or if he had any allergies at all. It seemed they knew just about as much about him as he did. The best he could do at this point was to give his name, rank, and I.D. number.

When he was rolled down this morning, he still had a ring on his finger; third finger, left hand. *Am I married, he wanted to ask?* Nurse Vaughn asked if he was able to remove the ring. She said it would be returned to him as soon as the testing was completed. She got a little metal bowl from the cabinet drawer, and walked over to the gurney. Either the patient was pretty weak, or the ring was stuck on his finger. Donna offered to help loosen it with a dab of Vaseline. Yes, it was on pretty tight. In a few slight twists the ring eased off his finger. She asked him when was the last time he had removed his ring, and he wasn't sure. *How stupid,* she thought, *why would you ask an Amnesia patient a question like that?* She could have kicked herself. With everything checked, and double-checked; her team was ready to go. Everybody was on point, and standing by. She gave her go-a-head, and left the rest to the professionals in Radiology. Not wanting to leave this piece of jewelry (*the upstairs attendants seemed to have forgotten to remove*) lying around, she picked up the dish, and took it back to her office with her for safekeeping.

Nurse Vaughn got started on her paperwork right away. If she was sure about anything, she was sure how easy it was to get behind in paperwork, and tied up in red tape. Amongst continuous updating, and training in her field of nursing, she had a new device to contend with, this *darn* new computer. This was the sixties, and modern technology was everywhere. It was easier for her to write down all the information on her office notepad first, and then transfer it to her computer. It was making two steps out of one her supervisor told her, but her reasoning was, if anything went wrong with these new fangled contraptions, at least she would have a back up. Besides, she didn't mind writing. She kept wonderful diaries. Donna started writing in a diary the week she came home with Lizzy. It wasn't an everyday thing, like a 'can't' do without it hobby. She just liked to write things down when something important came up in her life, or when interesting things would happen.

Donna did as much paperwork as she could do up to this point, and logged it in the computer, then decided to check on her patient. Everything was going according to schedule, and she went back to her office. She phoned the progress report upstairs to Dr. Al. When that was done, she saw she had time to take a short break. Her eyes fell on the ring in the metal dish, and she remembered she did not wipe it clean from the lubricant she used to get it off the patient's finger. She folded a tissue in half and carefully wiped it over the outside of the ring, and then on the inside where an inscription was, to make sure none of the Vaseline remained in the groves. Curiosity got the better of her, and she took a peek to see what was engraved in the band. If it was from his wife, she hoped it wasn't too personal to read. *Rachel.* She read the inscription again, this time aloud.

"Rachel. That's strange. I expected to see something a woman would say to a man, but this looks like he did this himself."

She was still squinting her eyes, reading aloud when she said the name again.

" Um, Rachel."

Her mind drifted to the only person she knew, named Rachel. That Rachel she met almost three years ago. Then she thought back. *Of course, the young girl I met was Amish, but she wasn't married.* Still, *why did I get this odd feeling in my stomach all of a sudden?* It's the same feeling I felt about two months ago when, out of the blue, Lizzy came to me, and said, Mommy, who is *Mamm?* I told her

I didn't know. I didn't particularly know anybody by that name, so I asked her where she heard it? She told me that nobody said it to her; that she just knew it all by herself up in here. Then, she pointed to her head. I didn't think much about it at the time, but I did think it odd enough for me to write in my diary.

The time had ticked away during Donna's reflecting, and it was time for her to attend to her patient. It may not mean anything at all, but she was sure that when she got home, she would inter the ring incident in her diary too. On her way down the hall, she pondered, *how much would this Robert remember of his past? Is he indeed married? Does he know the same Rachel I know? Is this girl his Rachel?*

"Oh my gosh, the ring." Donna stopped in her tracks, made an about face, and scurried back to her office.

chapter

NINE

This was something that Bill was truly not counting on. But, with Mrs. Yoder at home laid up with a sprained ankle, and him not being experienced enough to watch the store alone (even though he expected that Katie would come in and help), he had no other choice but to go to Walnut Creek with Mr. Yoder. What could he do? The wheels in his head were turning. He had to think of something fast. He knew he was the only one who could help Mr. Yoder, so he couldn't excuse his way out of the responsibility; besides, that's part of the reason he was hired in the first place. But, to ride to town sitting beside Mr. Yoder in an open market wagon was asking for trouble. Supposed he was to be recognized by someone. Suppose his beard, and mustache were not enough for his disguise? After all, the last time he was here he aroused suspicious questions in the minds of a couple of people who were close friends to Robert, and now to be going right into Walnut Creek within a mile of where the Millers lived, was taking a really big chance.

Just like that, an idea popped into his head, and it was a good one too. It wouldn't get him out of going, but it might help in more ways than one. He suggested to Mr. Yoder that he follow him there in a rental truck. If they got there and the furniture proved to be to much of a haul for the truck, or some of the good pieces needed a more secure holding than being tied to the open wagon with a rope, they would have the other truck on hand to meet the need. Bill suggested that because of the occasional dips, and grooves in the country back roads, the closed in truck would be sure to keep things from toddling over. It seemed like a good idea to Jonas Yoder. Plus, he was looking at the weather. The fee for the rental would not be that much extra, and they would only need the van for just that day, maybe less. It would work out fine. There was no problem with Bill renting the truck, he had a legal driver's licenses, and he would be the driver, because the Amish did not drive. If there was any drawback to the plan, it was that he wasn't going to get a chance to see Katie this morning. Originally, he would have been there with her and Mrs. Yoder. Aaron would have gone with his father. Katie didn't come in the store much to help out. He surmised she was doing most of the inside chores at home, but whenever she did come in; he noticed her. She was a pretty fair looking woman. He knew he had a few years on her, actually, about ten, or twelve, but he was sure she returned a pleasant smile at his greetings, whenever he would glance her way.

Plans on paper work out much easier than living them in real life. Somehow, *life* gets in the way. Today was moving day for Zack Zimmerman. His last visit to see Robert Jr. was near the beginning of the first part of the week. That was his goodbye visit. He thought it was best to wean himself, (so to speak), from the closeness he felt to Bobby. The visits had already become spurious, but knowing this was the last one made it even harder. I tried to busy myself at a distance, not wanting to stir up my own emotional feelings to their parting. Bobby had been fully mine for the last month and a half, and living here with me in the *Dawdi Haus*. We ate most of our meals with Mamm and Daed in the evening, and saw them everyday, but now it was Mr. Zimmerman who adhered to the agreement to limit his visits. He left his contact information with me, and said if I needed him for any reason at all; do not hesitate to call the number on the paper. It was the Mennonite neighbor's number who lived two farms over form his brother's.

Daed and Moses would be the ones going over to help load up the moving wagon. Mamm and Mrs. Miller had gone over yesterday to wrap the dishes and glassware in old newspapers, and properly pack them in boxes. Mr. Zimmerman was giving his wife's china set to me. He said he was sure that Laverna would have wanted it that way. The dishes were not things that I would need right away, so I asked Daed to store the boxes in the barn for now. I was satisfied using the few pieces that Mamm, and Elizabeth had given to me.

⮂

Bill paid the required down payment for the rental truck, and was on his way back to Jonas Yoder's hardware store. Things went as smoothly as he had hoped they would. His driver's licenses listed him as Bill Williams, and that's who he legally was. Mr. Yoder thought it would be too much of a traffic hazard if Bill tried following a horse drawn market wagon all the way to Walnut Creek, so he gave him written directions with posted landmarks on how to get him there. That was one of the things Bill was beginning to appreciate about Jonas Yoder, his thoughtfulness and his wisdom. If he had not already known the area from his past life here, these directions were right on point to get him to the Zimmerman place.

Bill knew the highway would get him to Walnut Creek faster, so he decided to take the long way around. He, remembering some of the Amish ways, understood; though people were cordial and friendly enough, he was still considered to be an outsider, an *Englischer.* So, for that reason he didn't want to arrive at the farm before Mr. Yoder did. He had met Zack when he came into the store to talk with Jonas. He only guessed it was about the move. Evidently, because he had his own wood working business, he not only had nice pieces to sell, but had a nice set of tools too. Bill often wondered what his life would have been like if he had come back home after his trouble. He knew he would have had the property, and the orchard, but he also wondered if he could have developed some other craft, or skill; something to put his hands to. The sun was high, but could change at any moment. He hoped it wasn't too chilly for the open market wagon. Most of the Amish and Mennonite had started to use their closed-in buggies in the past couple of weeks. It was close to the time for all of the hauling, and loading to be over with, and in the next week, or so, the open buggies would be put up for the winter.

Bill took the turn off to Sugar Creek. He could have headed straight for Walnut Creek, but he wanted to kill a few more minutes. Some of the area was beginning to look very familiar. He passed a couple of large farms that still had rolled bails of hay lying in the field. He felt a wave of nostalgia come over him as he got closer to what use to be home. *Mr. Yoder wrote in his directions that if I got to the Apple orchard, I had gone too far.* I had to smile to myself. Strasburg and Brewster I may not know so well, but Walnut Creek I knew like the back of my hand.

Katie could see that her Mamm and Mrs. Beiler were having a nice visit. They were sharing with each other things about their life; their personal likes and dislikes, the weather, food, and was on their way to exchanging some of their favorite recipes when she left the room. Katie wondered if this might not be a good time to mosey down to the store. Her brother Aaron could handle things on his own, but if it got a little busy, or an extra hand was needed, she would be available. Besides, she knew that Mr. Williams would be helping her Daed with the moving, now that things got turned around. The few times that Mr. Zimmerman came into the store to purchase things for his woodworking business, she saw the way Aaron, and Daed cut their eyes her way (in others words) seeking to see if she was interested in the newly widowed man. Katie's response was not to be mistaken. Her widen eyes, and the stern look on face said what she needed them know. **No!** She knew that as a lady who had once been married, there wouldn't be too many opportunities for her to marry again; except maybe to another widower, but in her mind, she dealt with low self esteem issues enough without being compared to another man's wife, especially this soon after her death. Some *'maidels'* have had a pretty rough time. The second time around they were used only to cook, be a cleaning woman, and to care for the widower's children. The tender love and care the new wife desires for herself, never happens.

When the love she thought she had in Enos Glick proved to be a horrible mistake, she was willing to stick it out, hoping his abuse would only be a temporary thing. But, it got to a point where it couldn't be hidden from the watchful eye of her mother. As a general rule, Amish parents did not interfere in the affairs of their offspring, but thank goodness that her Mamm and Daed did not stick to those boundaries. She had been married less than one year to Enos. *I guess I was too much in love,* she thought, *to admit that I saw some bad ways in him, even before we got married.* It didn't take long before the drinking became almost a daily ritual, and his visits into town to *that place* where you pay to see other women, was a weekly thing. She didn't say anything about her problem to anyone, because the wife usually got the blame. Maybe it was her silence, or her lack of joy as a newlywed that gave her away. It could have been that she was too silent at home. If she said anything to him, (even if it were a everyday jester) it caused trouble. If she was silent, that made him angry too. When she held her peace; she couldn't help but feel pity; not only him, but for herself too. It got so that anything was an excuse for him to become verbally, or physically abusive. Katie tried to stay hidden from people as much as she could because she was so ashamed of the mess she had gotten herself into. She was thankful for the traditional Amish clothing she wore. At least the sleeves covered her bruised arms, and the dresses came down to her ankles. It was her face she could not hide; not from bruises, or anything like that. It was her sad eyes. If she had only prayed to ask God if Enos was the right spouse for her, and waited on Him to answer. But no, she kept listening to wagging mouths saying her time was ticking away, and if she waited too much longer, she would end up a maidel. Well…she ended up a maidel anyway, and a widow to boot.

At that time April Yoder kept insisting that her daughter go to the bishop with her problem, but she was too afraid. She knew her Mamm just did not understand the kind of trouble she would be in when got home, if her husband found out she told the bishop about their private life. She had to pray to the heavenly Father and ask forgiveness for the many times the thought of doing her husband harm crossed her mind. She often wondered about other women going through similar situations, who had the courage to stick it out. *Nee, it wasn't all bad,* she thought. There were times when peace was in the house. Then thinking it over again, she remembered that those were the times when he was gone. Katie would redd-up the house, and make sure that everything was spotless, not that she was allowed to have it any other way. She'd cook a wonderful *gut* meal, but it all went unappreciated if Enos was in a drunken stupor when he got home. He would call her ugly names, and sometimes in a rage of temper, he'd sweep one arm across the table, and knock all the food to the floor. Then, he'd say, "You think I'm going to eat that slop? Look at this nasty house, there's crap all over the floor. Now get down on your hands and knees, and clean up that mess." Bitter, hurting tears would burn in the back of my eyes, and it took all that was within me not to strike out at him in a blinding rage. So, while I was down on my knees with tears flowing down my face, I decided it was a good time to pray.

I try not to dwell on the past, even though it was not that long ago. The news had come through the community of a *John Doe* whose buggy ran off the road, or was forced off the road by a passing vehicle. No one knew of it until the next morning. Evidently, the Amish buggy, and its driver were thrown over the embankment near County Line Creek. It was reported that the buggy was pretty smashed up, the horse was dead, and it took the authorities a while to find the driver. He had drowned. His body was caught between tree limbs that were not embedded that deep in the mud. The county sheriff's report said the victim had consumed a large amount of alcohol, and had it not been for that, he probably would have been able to free himself.

Since Daed and Mamm were preparing to move to Starks County to take over the hardware store that had belonged to his brother, I believed it was for me to go with them. I've learned that God works in mysterious ways, and who's to say what's right, or wrong if its God's own doing? As far as anybody here knows, I'm Katie Yoder, and I've never been married.

chapter

TEN

It wasn't that much of a distance to travel from Fort Dix, New Jersey to Lancaster, Pa., so Sergeant Baise took a few days of backlogged furlough. He needed time off, and the drive would do him good. Besides, he wanted to hand-deliver the information needed to identify the hospital's amnesia patient. This was the first real break the Army had in almost three years, and he didn't want anything to muff it up in any way. They weren't going to trust these personal documents going through the mail, sending them by an outside currier, or using that new Fax device.

By the time Robert had finished with all the scans, pokes, and inquiries, they had moved him from his temporary room to one on another floor. When his new nurse got him situated in bed, she asked if he needed anything to drink, or eat. He just wanted a little cup of water, no ice. On her way out the door, she let him know that the doctor would be in to see him soon, and that he had a couple of visitors with him.

Robert could not remember much of anything that might have happened to put him in the hospital. He was a bit confused. The two accidents were so closely related in location, that Dr. Al, and the hospital psychologist was anxious to see which incident would surface first. If it were the injury from three years back, or if it would be the accident from just two days ago, either way they were looking for possible memory blockage. The question was, had Robert William's memory been triggered to recovery because of the accident, or was it Jacob they would talk to? Since both injuries occurred in the same place, they weren't sure whom they would be dealing with. Dr. Al, his associate, and Sergeant Baise from the Army training camp, all left the doctor's office headed toward the elevator. They agreed that the two doctors would visit the patient first, as a matter of precaution. They wanted to observe first hand any memory retrieval that had taken place. The sergeant was to wait in the waiting room just down the hall, reserved for family.

When Sergeant Baise entered the waiting room, he saw an elderly couple sitting together on the small sofa. He assumed they were Mr. and Mrs. McAfee, the people Robert had been living with since he was assaulted and robbed. This would give him a chance to introduce himself, and to get acquainted with the couple. He thought they would appreciate hearing from someone who knew Robert before they found him, even if his association with the service had only been for a few short months. Meanwhile, the doctors would basically introduce a few questions inquiring about the patient's past history to determine what level of recovery had taken place. The psychiatrist would be observing his mental state, and charting his reactions while Dr. Al was doing a physical exam of his recovery from his accident. This would clue them in as to how they were to handle the three other guests waiting to see their patient.

Rachel thought about taking Bobby with her that Saturday of Zack Zimmerman's move, but decided against it. Maybe it wouldn't be such a good idea for him to pass by the house while things were being moved out. She didn't even know why she wanted to go by there, other than the fact to witness the finalization of another chapter in her life. Visiting the Miller's was a good excuse. Mamm agreed to watch Bobby. He was use to her by now, and Jacob was home, so he would be quite occupied. Mamm adored her grandchild, and so did Daed. Rachel felt that her son was becoming more hers every day. She didn't think that Bobby thought of Zack as his Daed any longer, although one can never be too sure of these things, but she did know that he had started to call him 'uncle Zack' a month or so back. It was because the Zook's had begun to call him by that name. His visits were fewer by then, and Rachel wondered if it saddened him as much as it did her.

"Ach", she said aloud, "Lord, You're the only guide I have. None of us have ever been down this road before. Help us to do it in the right way."

⁓

Nurse Vaughn sat at her kitchen table in her bathrobe, and slippers. It was her day off, and usually she slept in, but this morning, with coffee cup in hand, she sat reflecting on the happenings from the previous day. Admittedly, it wasn't the day that was so unusual; it was the patient and his ring that stirred her curiosity. She just couldn't get the name inscribed in the ring out of her mind. It probably would not have been anything to be anxious about, had it not been for the fact that when she called the hospital this morning to inquire about the young man, she was informed that he had been moved to a different floor. She also was told that the amnesia patient, Jacob McAfee, remembered his real name... *Robert Williams*. From that point on, her day had been altered. Donna tried to think about Lizzy's upcoming birthday party, and the little friends she had invited to share the day. Mrs. Vaughn took Lizzy for the whole day. They were going to eat out, pick up one of the presents Donna showed her mother she wanted to get for Lizzy, and then finish shopping for Thanksgiving dinner.

After her phone call to the hospital, Donna went to her bedroom. She opened the drawer to the nightstand beside her bed, and took out the two diary scrapbooks she'd been keeping every since she came home with Lizzy. Now that she was alone, a melancholy feeling came over her. She sat on the queen size bed, and opened one of the books. Two things happened on that cold winter day almost three years ago. She lost her own child who had come stillborn, and in the self-same day, God gave her Lizzy.

Donna remembered the eyes of the young Amish teenager. They were sad, and confused. It was not the norm, and certainly against department policy for the two young ladies to see each other, but it was by Donna's request that her friend, Mrs. Bell allow the mother to make this one and only visit to see her child. The young girl was not allowed to hold the baby, but Donna could not bear it if the girl could not look on her child's face one last time. The mother told her that she was going to name her daughter *Lizzy*, and if it wouldn't be too much trouble; could the baby keep that name. Donna promised her she would. It was plain to see that this was an unusual situation for Amish people to be in, and she was sure it was being done for reasons beyond the young girl's control. *Maybe even beyond the control of her family too.* The system did not allow the last name of the parents to be listed on the adoption papers, however the names Rachel, and Robert were listed as the birth parents.

The information she received from her earlier phone call was still racing through her head. *Robert,* she thought, *they said his name is Robert Williams.* Donna opened the dairy scrapbook marked number one, and looked at its first page. Her eyes slowly read down the page where they stopped on the typed words on Lizzy's birth certificate. She stopped at the space for the birth parents. It read: Father, *Robert. There was no last name.* Reluctantly, her eyes moved to the space for *Birth Mother.*

Donna slowly closed the book, and said in her mind, through tear stained eyes...*Rachel Zook.*

chapter

ELEVEN

Anna Zook had not discussed with her daughter the little treat she wanted to prepare for tomorrow night's supper. It would be Robert (Bobby's) third birthday on the following Monday, and she wasn't quite sure what Rachel would think about what she planned. It was just that Mr. Zimmerman was moving today, and Rachel may be a little distracted to have her mind on the upcoming event. Anna knew her daughter would not stop by the Zimmerman house to interrupt the men-folk with her presence, but over the last few years she had passed that house a many a day knowing God had placed her child there in someone else's care. It was soon to be a closing chapter in her life, and she wanted to pass by there one more time, just to thank God for the wonderful couple who was willing to be used for

His purpose. Robert Jr. could have been far removed like Lizzy was, so even through the pain of not being able to approach her son, she thanked God that he was just down the way, and every now and then she got a chance to peek at him out in the yard with Mrs. Zimmerman.

The days were getting colder, and the air was crisp. Rachel stopped by the shanty to telephone the Millers that she was coming for a visit. They knew the visit was more about seeing Tina, than to visit with them, but they didn't mind. Tina was home from college for the Thanksgiving break, and Rachel, though occupied with her own worries, wanted to hear more about this special someone that Tina had met at school. The real reason for the visit was because she didn't have any other friends to share things with. It would be Bobby's birthday on Monday, and although they didn't embrace having birthday parties, she wanted to invite the Millers over for dinner, that is if it was all right with her Mamm. It'll be kind of a reunion celebration she thought ... although some of the family will be missing. The sister-friends shared feeling after feeling, and when Rachel had stayed past her time, and was on her way home; she remembered she had forgotten about inviting them to dinner.

The packing and moving was going along at a good pace. Zack had plenty of help for the few things he had left. Mrs. Lillian Lapp was to come and get some special items for a family she knew that might be in need of them soon; the hand-carved infant cradle, and the little child's bed. Zack carved them himself. His wife had knitted, and crocheted a few new things once they knew they would be adopting one of the babies. The other baby items were from when they were expecting a 'wee' one of their own. He placed the bagged items in the cradle, put the cradle in the little bed, then stacked it all in the playpen, and sat everything near the kitchen door. Lillian bundled up in anticipation of the cold ride over to the Zimmerman's in the open market buggy. Usually by this time in November there were very few open buggies on the road. The Amish and Mennonite had reverted to their closed-in buggies for the winter season. But, for the short trip down to the Zimmerman's, which was less than a mile away, she would tuff it out.

Lillian, now a widower, asked one of her older sons to help with the drive, and the hauling. They turned the wagon into the yard, and came along side a rental moving truck. She knew Mr. Zimmerman was taking one suitcase for his clothes, and another one containing personal items from his marriage, so the truck must have been for the things going to Jonas Yoder's store, and she guessed, for whatever else he was delivering to Benjamin. There was one thing she knew, *for sure and for certain;* Mr. Yoder was not driving that truck. It must be that *Englischer* he has working for him. Lillian got down from the wagon to go inside the house. She knew her son would not let her carry anything, even if it was light. She just went along to make sure he picked up the right things. She let herself in the back door. No one was in the kitchen. So, she moved farther into the house.

"Hullo", she echoed.

There stepping out from behind a partially closed door was an Englischer. When she looked on his face, she stopped dead in her tracks. Whatever it was she was about to say went clean out of her head. If it had not been for the twenty odd years that had gone by, she could have been looking at Zeek Holfman come back to life. Realizing it was Lillian Lapp; Jonathan had almost the same reaction. He quickly placed his index finger to his lips indicating for her not to speak. He nodded his head toward the kitchen, placed his hand at her elbow, and gently walked into the large kitchen.

"Wie gehts!" "T'is Jonathan Holfman". He still held her arm to steady her.

"What the World!" was all she could say.

Jonathan could tell her voice was echoing do to the emptiness in the house, and motioned his head for them to step outside. By that time her son removed the folded blankets and rope from the market wagon, and was now coming through the door. Jonathan stood his distance, then went on through the kitchen door to the outside. Lillian, to nervous to speak, pointed to the cluster of furniture near the door. When she got her wind, she said she wanted to find Mr. Zimmerman to say her good-byes, and to see where the rest of the things were she had to get. Catching her eye outside the door, Jonathan nodded his head toward the little woodworking shop, and started across the yard. Seeing Mr. Zimmerman, Lillian thanked him again for all his kindness; wished him God's speed for his journey, and peace and prosperity for his upcoming life.

Then, she slipped by her son on one of his return trips back into the house, and dashed into the little workshop.

"As I live and breathe. T'is Johnathan Holfman."

"I'm sorry to put such a fright in you, Mrs. Lapp, I just didn't expect to run into anyone else who might recognize me. I've already been having a heck of a time trying to stay clear of Mr. Zook."

"But, what on earth are you doing here in Walnut Creek?"

"It's a long story, and we don't have much time to go into it now. Maybe I can explain it later. I was hoping my mustache and short beard would keep me from being noticed, but I guess it didn't work."

"It'll work just fine for those who didn't know your Daed, twenty-five years ago but, we were neighbors, and I must say, your disguise almost makes you the spitting image of him. It's a wonder Abraham Zook didn't pick up on it."

"Well, I'm not so sure I didn't peak his curiosity. I tried to avoid him as much as possible." Then, Jonathan said, "I think our time is out. I work at Mr. Yoder's store. I've been here for a couple of months, and I've been trying to stay away from faces that may recognize me. You'd better go before you are missed, and I'll get in touch with you by mail later on."

When Lillian turned to leave, Jonathan reached for her hand.

"Thanks for keeping me informed about my family all those years I was gone." Then he added..."and for praying for me too."

Lillian could feel a lump swelling in her throat. She gathered her winter shawl around her shoulders to brace herself against the cold, then, quickly said:

"God be praised", and rushed through the door towards the waiting wagon.

chapter

TWELVE

Dr. Al opened the slightly adjured door, and went in followed by the psychiatrist. The attending nurse had just entered her last observations, and medication information on the clipboard, and rather than replace it at the foot of the bed; handed it to Dr. Al Westly. He gave it a brief look over, and passed it on to the other doctor standing just to his left. Moving closer to the bed, he said,

"Well, how is our patient this morning?" being purposely careful not to mention any particular name.

The head portion of the bed had been raised, and the doctor started right in to taking the patient's vital signs, even though they had just been taken, according to the chart. The psychiatrist replaced the clipboard in its proper place, and moved to the other side of the bed. The doctor introduced his assistant, stating his medical credentials and why he had requested his presence. *Robert had no objections.* Still busy doing a thorough exam, the doctor reminded his patient, still not certain what name would surface, of his previous condition, and why they wanted to ask him a few simple questions. This was only to help them to determine the point of his recovery. He cautioned him not to be alarmed if things still seemed a bit foggy, or if he was not able to answer a specific question. The main thing was that, he didn't want him to strain, or fret over something that seemed unfamiliar to him. Actually, he thought the best route to go was to allow the patient to tell as much about himself as he could remember on his own, then they could decide where to go from there.

Sergeant Baise and Mr. and Mrs. McAfee were getting acquainted with each other in the waiting room. From what the older couple shared with him, Robert, or the man they called Jacob, was the same hard working, respectful recruit he came to know three years ago. A positive identification of the patient was declared the day before, however, the circumstances of his mental condition had not been determined. Physically, he was doing okay. The couple told the officer when they found Jacob he did not have a wallet on him, and he was not sure of anything. They said, if they took him to the emergency room, or called the police; that having no I.D. on him, the authorities might have thought he was a vagrant, or one of the homeless people, and take him to a shelter, but they somehow knew that wasn't his situation. It was something too well mannered about him. They took him back to their house, and Dessie suggested they call their family doctor. He was one of those who still made house calls. While they waited for him to come, Daniel had gone up to the attic to get some of the clothes that belonged to their son. The stranger looked to have been about his same size.

Mrs. McAfee went on to say the only possessions he had on him were the wedding ring, and a small key in the inside jacket pocket. Sergeant Baise' interest peaked up when she mentioned a key. He asked if the key was still available? If so, he'd like to have a look at it. Better yet, if Robert's memory was recovered, maybe he could say what the key belonged to. He was surprised that Mrs. McAfee had the key in her pocket. Just as Mr. McAfee thought a fresh round of coffee was due for all of them, Dr. Al walked through the waiting room door.

⌒⌒

This coming Monday, November 18, was Lizzy's birthday, so Donna decided to have her daughter's little party after church on Sunday. She didn't have too many people to contact. It would just be a few kids from her *'Wee Ones'* Sunday school class, her aunt, and her uncle on her mother's side. Aunt Dorian, was still single, and happy. She was a career woman and loved her work. According to her, she just never had the time, or the interest in getting married. Uncle Oscar was Mom's younger brother. He was married and had two girls. He had a very successful business. As a matter of fact, he franchised several men's clothing stores in the Philadelphia, Pa. area. It's kind of funny, because he always wanted to be the owner of a grand restaurant. Even though his girls are almost my age, I still invite him to everything because he's a fun-loving guy who enjoys being around family.

This is another *first* I'll have to put in my diary, because for the last two years, it was just Mom, Dad, and me celebrating Lizzy's birthday. Donna tried to feel upbeat about the party. She didn't know what was wrong. Maybe it was because the holidays were right around the corner, and all she had done so far was to pick out a matching coat and hat set for Lizzie. It was the sweetest little set she had ever seen. It was a bit too large for her now, but she resolved that by next year, Lizzy would grow into it right well. She just wasn't sure if it was going to be for her birthday, or for Christmas. Out of nowhere, her mind went back to the man in the hospital, and a funny feeling crept over her again. She didn't like it…and she couldn't make it go away. *'Just because this man could be Lizzy's father has no reflection on me. The terms of the adoption never stated that I had to give up my child if the father showed up, or if the natural parents got back together. Anyway,* she thought, *there are hundreds of Roberts and Rachels in this world. What's to say that the man in Lancaster General is the Robert on the birth certificate?*

Abraham Zook knew he wasn't acquainted with that many Englischers, yet there was something familiar about the man who drove the rental truck for Mr. Yoder. He couldn't quit put his finger on it, but it bothered him just the same; so much so that he mentioned it to his wife. Rachel had gone for a short visit to the Miller's. Abraham and Anna were glad whenever Tina Marie came home from college, because it gave Rachel a chance to socialize with someone her own age, and a good friend. She use to have another close friend, an Amish girl, but they seemed to have drifted apart about the time she stopped going to Sunday night 'Singings'. Since Anna wanted to get started with the evening meal, she was glad that Moses was home from school, that way, after his outside chores were done, he could keep a *'look see'* out for his brother, and his nephew when nap time was over.

Anna chattered away about how she wanted to have a little something extra in the way of celebrating Bobby's birthday. Now, she was well aware that the Old Order Amish, nor the New Order, for that matter, held to celebrating birthdays. But, with their newfound faith in Christ as Lord and Savior, they had broken with some of the old traditions. The traditions weren't all bad; it's just that some of them (she reasoned) must have been handed down from forefathers of a stricter time, that saw the need for certain decisions that would separate the *People* from the world. Many traditional ways from the *'Ordnung'* were never a set of written rules. They were just passed down by word of mouth. Maybe to be on the safe side she'd better not call this a party, but more of a special family dinner to say thank you to God for His great providence in all their lives these past three months...better said, these past three years. She also thought: *That's a mighty long explanation. Maybe I'd better shorten it a might.*

Coming back to the large kitchen table with several things in hand, Anna Zook wondered if her husband heard anything she was saying. Abraham sat gazing off into space. His eyes weren't really fixed on anything, but he'd stroke his beard every now and then and say, *"Umm, um, hum"*. She didn't take it that he meant to ignore her purposely, but she could tell he was deep in thought about something.

"Abe, Abraham, is anything wrong"?

Her husband turned to face her. He hadn't realized he was in such intense thought. It must have shown on his face.

"Oh, well, not really I guess. That is…I'm not sure."

Anna stopped with he biscuit making, wiped her hands on the corner of her black apron, and sat on the end of the wooden bench. Seeing the concern on her face, Abraham reached over and gave his wife's arm a loving pat.

"Nee, I didn't mean to give you an alarm. It's just that I saw someone today, an Englischer, who looked like someone we both knew a long time ago. I know it might sound *'narrisch'*– crazy, but he looked like Mr. Zeek Holfman, our old neighbor. As if he'd come back to life. The man was his spit'n image, only younger."

"Ach, that's *'lecherich'* ridiculous'!

"May be, that's what I told myself, but I know what I saw, and what bothers me more is, that he puts me in mind of someone else I know, only I just can't think of who that is right now. The only other man I 'spec that could favor him that much would have to be his son."

"Well, did ya say anything to the young man?"

"Oh, I greeted him, same as I would any other person. Other than that, didn't have much chance to speak to him. It may only be my imagination, but seems to me he tried prêt much to stay clear of me."

Looking up at the clock on the wall, Anna jumped to her feet pronouncing,

"Just look at the time. It seems like, *The hurrier I go, the behinder I get"!*

The both of them let out a 'tee hee', and she dove back into her biscuit making, while Abraham turned another page in his paper, and continued to think over the stranger's face. Meanwhile, Anna thought to herself, *there's been so much scurrying around this weekend; maybe I'll just wait to have the little celebration for Sunday. That way Elizabeth and Ben can come with their little family, and maybe Ruthie could come with Rosie.* It all sounded like it would work out just fine, except she thought again; Mary might have to bring Rosie by. I wouldn't want to stir up any trouble for Ruthie and her husband because of our shunning.

chapter

THIRTEEN

Dr. Al Westly took a comfortable chair between his waiting visitors. He had wonderful news for all involved. As a matter of fact, it was none short of miraculous. It seemed by their physical observation, the patient was experiencing a one hundred percent recovery. However, he used the word *seemed* with caution. Dr. Westly told them one could never be certain of these things until one got farther down the road in his recovery. The psychiatrist stipulated that this was a crucial pivoting point, and the worst thing that could happen right now would be to overload the patient with an influx of information for him to recall. From what they could determine at this time, Robert's recall recovery included his months in the Army, some of his stay with the McAfee's, and his injury three years ago. What could not be determined at this point was if he was aware of the length of time that had occurred between the two incidents. They had to wait and see what he remembered about his immediate family relationships. Because they now were certain of a positive ID, the next step would be to contact his family in Walnut Creek. The authorities at Fort Dix, and the Bureau of Missing Persons would determine how to go about that.

The doctors thought they would start with the last, and possibly the more familiar faces Robert would remember. That's why they wanted Mr. and Mrs. McAfee to visit the room first. Dr. Westly also reminded them that when Jacob came to himself (so to speak) he did say that his name was Robert Williams, and not Jacob; so for all intents and purposes, he may recognize them as the people he lived with, but not necessarily respond to the name Jacob. They would just have to play it by ear. If they got thrown off tract, or needed any help adjusting, the psychiatrist would be in the room with them. Meanwhile, he and Sergeant Baise would concentrate on notifying his uncle and aunt in Walnut Creek.

Daniel and Dessie walked down the hall and located the nurse's station to announce whom they were visiting. Their names must have been listed on the paper the nurse pulled out from what appeared to be some sort of login book. They were given a pass that had his room number on it written in black marker pen. Mrs. McAfee thought to herself; *it was good they had people to give them directions from place to place; otherwise they would have been lost.* A few doors down the corridor, but still in view of the nurse's station, they located the room. They both stood for a few seconds before going in. They read the note posted on the door. **IMMEDIATE FAMILY AND AUTHORIZED PERSONNEL ONLY!** Dessie heard her husband take a deep breath as they pushed the large door open and entered the room. They were so nervous. What would Jacob's reaction be? The other physician, who had been seated at the time, rose when they came in. He addressed his statement to Robert.

"Ah! I see you have a couple of visitors Robert." His slightly raised eyebrow was just a friendly reminder of the name change. Then he took his seat again.

Daniel indicated with his nod that he understood the unspoken hint. Robert's face brightened, and a smile lit the corners of his lips as the couple approached the bed. At that instant a surge of panic waved through Dessie's mind, and she couldn't part her lips to say hello. She didn't know what to do. She gripped her husband's arm a little tighter and a tear began to trickle down her cheek. Luckily, Robert spoke first.

"Hi folks." He could see the water overspill in her eyes.

"No need to cry Mrs. 'D', they tell me I'm going to heal up A-okay, and not just from the fall, but with my memory loss too."

Now a full flood of tears escaped her. Mr. McAfee drew closer to the bed, and patted Robert on his good shoulder, while his wife fished in her purse for a handkerchief. She then moved closer to the bedrail, and leaned in to give him a big kiss on the cheek, and looking up towards the ceiling, and with both hands raised in the air said:

"Hallelujah, hallelujah. Thank you Jesus!"

"Praise the Lord", Daniel said. "Now calm down Momma, we don't want to upset the whole hospital."

He lowered his head to look over the rim of his glasses at Robert, and arching his eyebrows, and widening his eyes, said:

"You know how excited Momma can get." Daniel McAfee looked at the puzzled expression on the physician's face.

"Ya see" Daniel said, "Mr. and Mrs. 'D' is the nickname Jacob has, or had for us. My name is Daniel, and my wife's name is Dessie Rea. Our boy here, that's what we call him, *our boy,* thought it endearing to show his closeness to us by calling us Mr. and Mrs. 'D', since we weren't his real parents. And that young man is why my wife was crying. Because, no matter if he's Robert, or Jacob, he remembers us, and we're sure everything is going to be all right."

They wanted to stay longer, but kept their word to having a short visit. They wanted their *boy* to know they would be close at hand if he needed them for anything at all; just have the hospital to call. The couple eased out of the room, and stood in the corridor for a minute, or two. They just wanted to embrace each other in the realization that Jacob had come back, but knowing it was Robert who would soon be going home...out of their lives.

chapter

FOURTEEN

Pastor Quincy Folks came to Lighthouse Christian Ministries almost five years ago. He was acting as interim after the death of Pastor Matthews. At that time he was only twenty-nine years old, and was the youngest pastor the congregation ever had. Some congregants expected radical changes to take place, and others hoped to keep things as they were. Had it not been on an almost deathbed request by Pastor Matthews himself for him to consider the position, Quincy Folks would have looked for an assignment somewhere else. He would soon be thirty-four years old and longed to meet the wife he knew God had for him. The work was growing, and aside from desiring a *helpmate,* he admitted to spouts of loneliness, and being a single pastor in a growing congregation these days, increased that level of stress. Even so, on some Sundays, he found himself making a mad dash to his office as soon as the benediction was said. It was the only way for him to avoid certain young ladies who might be headed his way for idle conversation, and flirtation.

However, his eye did fall on a particular young lady in the congregation. She was the daughter of Deacon and Mrs. Vaughn, sister Donna. He didn't know any intimate details about her personal situation of being a single parent, but he knew from observing her in church these past few years, that she loved the Lord, she was faithful, a good worker, and above all, she was not a *busy body!* He purposely tried to catch her eye a couple of times, hoping for a friendly smile back, but wasn't quite sure if it worked or not. Actually, he liked her very much; which now was one of the reasons he held off on sharing the *Word* he heard from the Lord, concerning her. It came to him a couple of days ago when he was praying for the congregation, and he knew he had to speak it to her. He didn't want God to see him as a slowful servant.

During the *Holy Hug* time, Pastor Quincy made sure the note to see him in his study after service was delivered to Donna by one of his assistants. She was a beautiful, confident young lady, and he hoped that what he had to say to her was something that the Lord had already spoken to her in her spirit. He asked the church secretary to remain after service until he finished his meeting with sister Vaughn.

Donna could not imagine why Pastor Quincy wanted to speak with her. She really didn't have much time to dilly dally around today. Lizzy's birthday party was going to be at four O'clock, and there were still a few things to do. She had driven her own vehicle to church, because she had a stop to make on the way home. Since this unexpected meeting came up, she asked her parents to take Lizzy on home with them. The look on her mother's face asked a question that she couldn't answer. She just hunched her shoulders, and returned her mother's look with a questioning one of her own. Donna tapped on the open church office door, saying that Pastor Folks wanted to see her. The church secretary, Mrs. Daily motioned for her to sit in one of the empty chairs in front of her desk, leaving to announce her arrival. She popped back through the door in a few seconds, and told me the Pastor would see me now.

Quincy Folks stood and moved from behind his desk when Donna entered the room. He had to look at her face while extending his right hand, but hoped he didn't dwell there too long. *Gosh,* he thought, *She sure is beautiful.* He offered her a seat, and sensing the need for one of his own, quickly moved back to the chair behind his desk. He cleared his throat, and reminded himself that he was taking care of business for the Lord...*not for Quincy Folks.*

"Well, sister Vaughn, I suppose you're wondering why I asked to see you?"

"Yes sir. Have I done anything wrong?"

"Wait a minute (he said with a smile). Let's back up a bit. First of all, it would make me feel a lot more comfortable if we dispensed with the 'Sir' part. And, why is it when people are summoned to the pastor's office, they assume it's because they've been out of line?"

Before she could answer, he leaned forward, and said: "You haven't done anything wrong, have you?"

"What? I mean, No. I hope not."

He was smiling very broadly, and the Holy Spirit nudged him again to get to the point.

"Relax, relax, he said. You haven't been called to the principal's office. It's just that in my time of prayer, I believe the Lord gave me a *'Word'* to share with you."

Donna relaxed and let a slight smile cross the corner of her lips. He tried not to notice her slightly parted lips, and perfectly aligned teeth. *Man! I didn't know that I was going to be this distracted.* He gave himself a mental slap across the face, and moved on.

"Sister Vaughn, as a pastor, I'm always praying for those whom I have charge over, asking God to meet their every need. Well, in doing so; I believe God gave me a special *'Word'* for you."

Donna sat there stirring. *What in the world could God have to tell him about me?*

"What I believe I heard from the Lord was this: *"Because you have been a good steward over that which I have loaned you, I will give to you the desire of your heart".*

Donna sat motionless. Quincy could not tell in searching her face if she was in shock, or just stunned, but whatever it was, it must have impacted her very hard.

"Sister Vaughn, sister Vaughn. Are you alright?"

He was glad he asked Mrs. Daily to stay. He usually would have dialed her special ring tone from his desk phone, but he was too nervous to think of her code. He called out across the hall, and told her to bring a cup of water for sister Vaughn, and please hurry! He had already moved from behind his desk, and was standing at Donna's chair. He took one of her hands in his, patting the back of it with his own.

"Oh, my goodness! Donna, are you all right?" He completely forgot the 'sister' part.

Hearing Mrs. Daily coming from down the hall, he let her hand go, and placed his hand at the back of her right shoulder. Pastor Folks waved frantically for his secretary to come quickly with the water.

"Oh, mercy, what in the world?" she said heading towards the young lady who was still in some kind of a daze. "Here dear, take a few sips of this water."

She placed the paper drink cup in Donna's hand, and helped to steady it as she drank. After a couple of sips, Donna lowered the cup, and tried to regain her composure. Putting her hand on her forehead, and speaking slowly she said,

"I'm alright, I think. I don't know what could have caused me to react that way."

"Are you sure you're all right", he asked? His voice was loaded with compassion.

"Yes Sir, I was just…I was just."

What was she? She didn't even know what she was saying.

Poor Pastor Folks had such a weird, but concerned look on his face. And as for Mrs. Daily, who wasn't sure if the girl was ill, or if she needed more attention; was not about to leave her in the hands of Pastor Quincy, *who must have been the culprit behind whatever it was that just happened to her!* Pastor Folks gave Mrs. Daily a nod of dismissal. She walked backward to the door, but not without first giving him the cautious look of a protective mother hen that said: *You very well may be the pastor, but you're still a man, and I'm keeping my eye on you.* He had no idea why the *Word of knowledge* should have affected her like it did, but he was awfully happy he didn't deliver it to her in the open sanctuary setting, as he first planned. It was the Holy Spirit who prompted him to do otherwise.

Donna felt a little embarrassed because she allowed herself to react the way she did. *Even though deep down inside, she really did know why. It was a loud confirmation of what she felt the Lord was telling her in her heart.* She then, assured the pastor that she was okay, and put a smile on her face. She stood, extending her hand. Quincy was thrown off guard. He shook her hand, and offered her one of his cards, saying if she needed anything at all, to please give him a call. He knew that if she did not call him before Wednesday, he would call her. She explained that her daughter's birthday party was today, and she must get home to finish preparing for it. Donna peeked her head in the church office door, and thanked Mrs. Daily for her assistance; then she left.

chapter

FIFTEEN

Sergeant Baise spoke with Robert for just a few short minutes after the McAfee's came out. He asked the couple if they could wait for him in the private waiting area where they were before, and he would catch up with them there.

Robert remembered Sergeant Baise well, but the timeframe was a bit foggy. Outside in the corridor the psychiatrist explained that right now, Robert was experiencing partial recovery. He would remember things like boot camp training, only to him, it could seem like last week. His memory connection hooked right up to the McAfee's, and, yes he knows some time went by while he was there, but since it was spent as Jacob McAfee, not Robert Williams, there's a void. In hind-sight, there is a three and a half year gap for Robert, so one would have to be careful how they approach, and present information to him. When the sergeant returned to the waiting room, he got the key from Mrs. McAfee. She said she had no idea how it might have helped in his situation, but she brought it along anyway. He said he would do some investigating, and get back in touch with them later. Looking at the key, he was sure it was nothing that was Army issued, so maybe it was to a personal safe, or locker. He thought he would start where they last knew Robert to have gone... the Lancaster train station.

⌒⌒

The late afternoon sun was still at its peak around three o'clock in the afternoon when Rachel left the Miller's house. She had gone to visit with Tina Marie, and to extend an invitation for them to come for Thanksgiving dinner. Traditionally the Amish did not have big family gatherings for Thanksgiving, or Christmas. Still, they always prepared a bountiful meal for their immediate families. She was just as much a part of the Miller family now as they were a part of hers. However, she found that her family had been invited to the Miller's and the ladies of each household planned to combine their prepared dishes to put together one big meal. Up until then, she never realized how accepted she was by the Miller's as part of their family.

Rachel still had melancholy feelings whenever she passed the phone shanty, but today walking past the Zimmerman's empty farm made her feel more lonely than ever. Her Daed told her that Mr. Zimmerman was going to spend his last night (tonight) in town at a motel, so he could get the early train to Lancaster in the morning. Now, thinking of the early morning train reminded her of the last time she saw her beloved. With every step, she felt as if she were shrinking into nothingness, and wondered if by the time she reached home, if she would be able to even climb up the back stoop.

Anna Zook could tell when her daughter got in, she was feeling somewhat depressed. She was hoping the visit with Tina Marie would have brightened her mood a little. Maybe her news about having a little birthday celebration for Bobby would do the trick. At any rate, she had to take a chance that it would, because she had already invited Elizabeth and her family. Little Abe, and Bobby got along so well together, and the two little darlings didn't see each other nearly enough. Everything could be ready by this evening, so there wouldn't be much to do tomorrow when they got back from service. The Zook's often visited the little Baptist Church the Miller's attended, and they also visited the Mennonite (almost fully Christian now), church that Ben and Elizabeth attended. They felt equally comfortable at both places. Anna asked her husband if they could attend the Miller's church for tomorrow, only because it was closer. The weather was changing so, and it would take less heated bricks for the trip in the closed-in buggy. Besides, she thought, it would give them an opportunity to sit in fellowship with the other side of the family, which technically, they were.

Anna enjoyed the message, and the lively music. Singing aloud for pleasure was an Amish 'no, no', but somehow it almost came naturally to Anna. That was one of her well-kept *secret sins* from the past; something she often asked forgiveness for. She would hear a melody in her head, and had no idea where it came from, except from inside her heart. Now, with Christ in her life, she no longer had to repent, or feel ashamed when words of a lovely hymn floated to her mind. Anna especially enjoyed the hymn sung in service today, 'Bringing In The Sheaves'. She was a giver at heart, and one who always extended her hand to help those in need, and in a way the song was telling a story about people who did just that. This coming week would be Thanksgiving, and when they were at church, Norma Jean asked if the Zook's could share the dinner at her house, instead of hers. Anna was delighted. This would be their first Thanksgiving of this kind.

Bill was torn between attending the Christian Church service at Pastor Beiler's, and going over to the Amish service with the Yoders. He knew he was free to go wherever he wanted to go. He also knew that if he went to the Amish service it would be because he wanted to see Katie Yoder. He had looked forward to seeing her the day before at the store, but because of her mother's accident, things got shifted around. He ended up going to help Mr. Yoder with Mr. Zimmerman's move, and Aaron was the one to stay in town and look after the store. He was pretty sure that Katie caught his eye contact a couple of times. Of course, being Amish she wouldn't be so bold as to say anything to him, especially since some of her hurt, he understood, came because of her deceased husband and an Englischer. Still, he didn't think that would be as much of an obstacle as the difference in their ages. With him nearing his mid-forties, he knew he had at least twelve to maybe even thirteen years on her. *Well, even so, I haven't felt this way about a woman in ages; every since my wife died. This is the first woman I've really been drawn to.* God had been so merciful to him, he didn't know how to ask Him for one more thing.

My main purpose in coming here was to find my son. It's been almost three years since our eyes locked on the street, and at that train station. He began to pray. *Lord, I know I'm in the right place, at the right time. It wasn't in my mind to find a wife, but you know everything I need. Please give me patients, and the courage to wait until You make Your move. Amen.*

chapter

SIXTEEN

The telephone rang right after dinner just when Norma Jean was clearing the table, so Ezekiel Miller answered it. After his hello, there was a pause, and then he said:

"Is this some kind of a joke? Who is this?" he demanded.

The voice on the other end of the line said,

"This is Sergeant Anthony Baise of the United States Army, and I assure you sir, this is no joke!"

On her way back into the dinning room to get another handful of dishes from the table, Norma Jean glanced toward her husband who was still on the telephone. His face looked like he had just seen a ghost. She sat the dishes back on the table, and in a few quick steps was at her husband's side.

"What is it, she said, what's wrong?"

"Yes", her husband was saying to whoever was on the other end of the receiver.

"I see." Then he said, "I don't believe it! Praise the Lord, Praise the Lord!"

Norma Jean was on pins and needles. "What is it, she said. What's happened?"

Ezekiel Miller kept nodding his head in response to whatever was being said to him on the other end of the line.

"Yes. Okay...okay...sure will."

Then he covered the receiver, and told his wife to go get a pencil and a piece of paper. She went quickly to the dinning room buffet cabinet, opened the drawer that held the items, and rushed back with them. Ezekiel waved his hand indicating for her to write down what he was being told.

"Okay I'm ready, Amtrak from Strasburg to Lancaster. Yes. We've got it. Someone will meet us there, and take us to the (he indicated for her to write again) hotel on Harrisburg Pike. Um hum, it's a few blocks from there to Lancaster General. Yes sir, yes sir. Thank you again, and we'll see you tomorrow afternoon. Goodbye"

Before he could say another word, he ran, and plopped in one of the living room chairs. Tears streamed down his face. Norma Jean didn't know what to do. Her worst fear had come true...*They've found Robert's body.*

My God, My God, she thought. She was trying to make her way to the sofa before her legs gave way. Ezekiel saw the frightened, drained look on his wife's face, and ran to her aid.

"Honey...No, no, it's good news. They've found Robert. He's alive! He's alive."

Tina Marie heard the commotion in the living room. She wiped her hands on her apron, and darted through the open dinning room entrance. Her parents told her the news, and they all had a good cry of rejoicing and praise. When their spirits had calmed, Mr. Miller filled them in on as much as he knew of the remarkable event. Now, came the hard part. They were not to tell anyone. Not even a close relative. He said the Army understood that other people were very much involved in Robert's life, however, the two of them were being called in to...well, to sort of officially identify that the person in the hospital room was indeed Robert Williams. Until the Millers had made a positive I.D., the government officials would not release any public information. They were very cautious about what the news media would do with misinformation.

Because Robert had missed about three years from his life back in Walnut Creek, he would need to be filled in slowly. Norma Jean always tried to hang on to a shred of hope. She also tried to visualize how she would feel when Robert was finally found. This feeling was not even close to what she imagined. It was so much more. In quoting words from a familiar hymn she said, *"My God moves in mysterious ways, His wonders to perform; He plants His footsteps in the sea, and rides upon the storm"*

Tina went up to her room with mixed emotions. The cloud of secrecy the family was sworn to keep dampened the happiness of her cousin being found. The thankfulness in her heart was diminished by the depressing gloom that arose there. She was crushed that she could not share the news with the one who may have needed to hear it more than all of them…Rachel. Tina drove her parents to the train station early the next morning. The Army offered to fly them into Lancaster, but by the time they could drive to an airport close enough to them, fly to Philadelphia, get picked up, and be driven to Lancaster, it would have possibly taken just as long as the train ride. Tina saw her parents safely off, but on the drive back home, thought of something going on in the big city that her parents were not very use to…the Civil Rights Movement. She didn't mean to sound like she was not for the Movement, because she was. It was just that this was her parent's first opportunity to stay in a hotel, and she hoped that whatever was going on; it would not prevent them from staying in the hotel that Sergeant Baise had selected for them. She wanted their stay to be enjoyable, but she also wanted them to be safe. They were under enough pressure as it was.

Donna tried to enjoy the rest of her day at Lizzy's birthday party. Her mind kept getting preoccupied with the conversation she had earlier with pastor Quincy. Maybe a three year old would not notice anything different, but her mother sure did. After the celebration was over, and all the company had gone, Mrs. Vaughn approached her daughter. Lizzy was in the living room happily playing with Grandpa, and her new presents. Mrs. Vaughn did not interfere with Donna's life as an adult, but as a mother, she could see that something was bothering her daughter, and whatever it was, happened today between church and home. They sat in the kitchen for a 'mother-daughter' talk.

Her mother told her it wasn't just the immediate quandary, but she noticed that for the past few days she seemed to have distanced herself from the inner circle of the family.

Donna knew what she was about to share with her mother would have an effect on the entire family. She told her mother the *'Word'* pastor Quincy had given her, and then she shared what had happened over the last few days at the hospital. Donna was already crying, and said if it were true, how could God ask such a thing of her? Mrs. Vaughn suggested that if it were possible, for her to pray to God out of her *faith,* and not out of her fear. She also asked Donna to reflect on the many times in the Bible where God tested parent's faith, not just to give their children away, but at times to even offer them as a sacrifice. Not as an *Idol* worshipper, but like in the case of Abraham, to test his faith. This, of course, was not something that Donna eagerly wanted to hear, but she told her mother she would pray and ask God to search her heart.

❧❧

That Sunday morning at church, before the phone call had come that afternoon about Robert, Mrs. Miller told Anna she would try to come by for her special setout for Bobby. She had prepared dinner, and still wasn't sure if Eli and his family would drop by, or not. Norma Jean gave Anna a small box wrapped with paper that had *Happy Birthday* on it. It was a gift for Bobby, just in case they could not make it over to the party. She told her it wasn't much, just a little wind-up toy, and she first thought about saving it for a Christmas present. She even thought to give it to him when they shared their Thanksgiving dinner together, but she didn't want Bobby to get confused as to what they were celebrating. They both had a small chuckle about that.

The Zook household was filled with chatter, and the pitter-patter of little feet. The other men-folk stayed home. Elizabeth brought little Benjamin-Abraham, and Aendi Mary came with Rose Ann. She thought it best if Ruthie not cross the sensitive line of her relative's shunning, since her husband remained with the Amish church. Jacob was a little older than the others, but was no less excited. All the little cousins were running around, so happy to see each other. This was the first gathering of its kind for them. We really didn't name it, but they knew it was just a special gathering for the little people, and after the dinner, they were going to have ice cream and cake. Anna would save back the gift that Mrs. Miller gave for Bobby until after the company had gone home. Other than that, there were no gifts to be given. Anna was busting with joy. She told Mary and Elizabeth that her household was going to do something very unusual for the Thanksgiving meal too. She told them it would be another 'first' for them, and for some odd reason (she didn't know why), she felt the two families should share their thankfulness together this year.

The evening went well, and every one had a good time. When Rachel was tucking Bobby into bed for the night, she prayed over him in her usual manner. The surprise gift lay next to him on top of his quilt. He looked so tuckered out. She thought the long day had been too much for him.

"Are ya alright sweetie", she asked. Did ya enjoy having all your cousins over today?"

"Jah"

"Are you too tired for a night time story?"

"No Mamm, but I wished my friend could have come today."

Rachel thought for a second. Friend, what friend? "But, all our cousins were here today honey."

"Nee, not those *Mommy*, the little girl."

"What little girl. Do you know a little girl?"

She thought, maybe it was one of the little toddlers from church.

"Jah", he said. "Sometimes we see each other and smile, and sometimes I see her from when I wake up."

Rachel realized he must be talking about a make believe friend again, or someone in his dream. Some children, who don't have other siblings to play with, think up make believe friends. Rachel went along with his fantasy.

"I'm awfully sorry your little friend couldn't come. Maybe we can invite her to something else."

"Oh, that's okay Mommy, she had a birthday party today too. She got a toy, and a pretty new coat."

"Well, that's nice sweetie", she said, Now, what story would you like for me to read to ya?"

Rachel lay in bed awake pondering over what Bobby said to her at bedtime. A couple of things troubled her; one, the little girl's birthday party was today. That may not have been so strange, except for the fact that, they never called his little celebration a birthday party. And, then he was very specific about her getting a coat. The strangest thing of all was, at least two times he called me '*Mommy*', not '*Mamm*'. Giving way to sleep, she wondered, *could his little make believe friend be English?*

chapter

SEVENTEEN

Quincy Folks sat in the oversized recliner in his bedroom. He reflected on the day. Most people, he surmised, were turning out their lights, and saying their goodnights, but for him, it was his usual time for prayer, and meditation. Except, tonight he couldn't concentrate. His mind kept wondering. He was thinking on his meeting with sister Vaughn. He was not questioning God about what he delivered to Donna. It was her unexpected reaction that threw him off. Putting the pastor in him aside for a moment, he was also a man, a man who cared about this woman very much. He often wanted to make a move (so to speak) to take the initiative to begin a personal relationship with her, but the timing was never right. And now, he thought, I actually get the chance to sit with her in my office, and what happens…I make her cry. He shook his head, and smiled to himself. *Lord, I may be a bit rusty at this finding a mate thing, but it seems to me that causing someone to go to pieces, and causing them to possibly hate you for the rest of your life, doesn't appear to be making a very good first impression.* Then Quincy spoke out loud, "Forgive me for not doing a very good job of praying for the sheep tonight, but this is one shepherd who needs Your help. I've got Donna on the brain!"

When Sergeant Baise left the hospital that morning, he headed straight over to the Amtrak station with the key Mrs. McAfee gave him. Sure enough, it was one of their keys. The problem was, the key no longer fit locker 917. He went to the office, and they explained that when they find that a certain key hasn't been returned, or used for a while, they change the lock. If anything is in the locker, the items are inspected. Most things are discarded, and others are taken over to lost and found. In this case, he hoped it was the latter. After showing his ID, and answering a few questions, he was escorted to the lost and found. It was no bigger than a bedroom closet. Fortunately, there were only a few items on the shelves. He spotted two small bags, neither one was Army issued, and hoped that one of them belonged to Robert Williams.

The office personnel said he had no sure way of tracking how long these items had been in the lost and found, but he knew it had to be for at least a year; maybe longer. Things could have been in the locker for up to a year before they emptied them. Sergeant Baise stood there

thinking for a minute. Wait a minute. Of course! The bag
I'm looking for wouldn't be an Army bag. That would
have been left at the Base. Robert wasn't going home,
he was taking a day of furlough. He looked in one of the
small travel bags. What luck! It belonged to Robert. This
was to good to be true. It had personal letters he had written and received, socks, a pair of casual shoes, some other
things, and something that seemed a bit odd to him; a
small bottle of *Blue Waltz* cologne.

He signed for the bag, and left the station. He put
the bag in the trunk of his car to be certain he had it when
he went back to the hospital. These personal possessions,
and the key from Mrs. McAfee strongly identified this
man as the missing Robert Williams. When the Miller's
got in on Monday and formally identified him, the military could release their statements to the media. Although
Sergeant Baise wasn't necessarily a very religious man, a
phrase from a song of his childhood passed through his
mind. *"I once was lost, but now I'm found..."*

All went well with the Miller's travel. They called
Tina when they got to the hotel. They quickly took out
what they needed to freshen up with, so they could be
down in the hotel lobby when the liaison arrived. Both
of them were nervous, although they tried not to show it.
Mr. Miller felt like pacing the floor, but thought it better
that he sit with his wife. He didn't want to look like a
crook casing the joint.

The ride over to the hospital was short. They were
to meet first with the two doctors who were taking care

of Robert. Normal visiting hours in that wing of the hospital ended at 7:00pm, but they were given special permission by administration to see Robert. The escort delivered them to a small waiting area to meet with the doctors. After the introductions, Ezekiel and Norma Jean were given more information about what had happened to their nephew over the past three years. They were told of any improvements in Robert's condition that may have occurred since the initial phone call. The military had even recovered a satchel that helped to identify him, and the doctors talked positively about his full recovery. Dr. Al filled them in on the McAfee's, and said they would have an opportunity to meet them the next day at their home. They thought it best that the Millers should visit Robert alone, to cut down on any confusion that might take place between them and the McAfees. They were told that Robert would know them, and all his connections to them in the past, what they were not sure of was how he would handle *the reunion*. Like anyone who has been away for a long period of time with no inside contacts, he was not expected to have any recollection of what has been going on in Walnut Creek since his departure. They were to answer his questions as truthfully, and fully as possible, but if any notable signs of strain, or confusion appeared, they were to discontinue along that track.

Doctor Al tapped on the door, and pushed it slightly ajar.

"Hey buddy", he said, "I know it's getting near your suppertime, but are you ready for the visitors I promised you?"

"You bet!"

That was Robert's voice. Norma Jean would know it anywhere. They fished for each other's hand, and entered the room. Maybe the both of them had expected to see the same thing; a frail, skinny, small framed boy laying in the bed, but the man sitting in the chair was not the Robert they *had* embedded in their memory. This man was well developed with muscular arms, and broad shoulders. He was not the nineteen-year-old boy who left their house three and a half years ago. The man who rose from the chair was at least three inches taller than their nephew. Norma Jean always wondered how she would react when she saw her Robert again. *Maybe this was the wrong man, a mistake in identity.* Her grip tightened on her husband's hand. The silence was broken when Robert moved toward them.

"Hey, what is this? I thought I was the one suffering from Amnesia. Uncle 'Zeek', Aunty Jean, don't you recognize me?"

He drew her close, and gave her a big hug, kissed her on the cheek, then vigorously shook his uncle's hand, patting him on the back with the other. He stepped back, smiling that wonderful smile that belonged to him along. It hit them both at the same time. *Oh, my God! It's Robert.* Robert could read the look on their faces.

"Hey, you folks look like you need a seat. Better yet—

He poked his head outside the room, and looked down towards the nurse's station. He waved his hand a few times in the air to get Dr. Al's attention. He knew he would be close by.

"Dr. Westly." Robert motioned for him to come down to the room. "Look Doc, I want to sit with my folks, and there's only two chairs in the room. Can I get another chair?"

He wanted to make it as easy for Robert as he could, so he said:

"Hold on for a minute, I've got a better idea."

He went back to the desk to see if it was okay for them to use the little private waiting room. It was. He told Robert to put his robe on, and he would be right back. He went the short walk down the corridor to the waiting room where the liaison and Sergeant Baise was waiting. He asked them to go across the hall to sit in the vending machine area, but he asked Sergeant Baise to leave the satchel on the floor close to the wall. With everything in order, he went back around the corner, and waved them toward the room. He explained that he would be just outside the door if they needed him for anything. Regulations required that the door not be closed, so he sat in a folding chair, within earshot of everything that was said. The Miller's were still in disbelief, but Ezekiel broke the ice.

"You must forgive us Robert, but you look so different from the boy we said goodbye to us at the Amtrak station a few years ago. You're so grown up, so mature."

Robert smiled. "I guess I owe that to Boot Camp, and Uncle Sam. Of course, living with the McAfees' for the past few years caused me to work a lot of odd jobs, you know, because of not having proper I.D. like a driver's license, or birth certificate. They are good Christian folk, *'Old school'*, strong believers in: if you don't work, you don't eat!"

"Thank goodness for that", Ezekiel said. Mrs. Miller wanted to join in the conversation, but all she could muster up was, "My, my, my, my, my, I just can't believe it."

Robert had been holding back a question that the doctors, the McAfees, nor Sergeant Baise could answer. It had been in his head for the last four days, ever since his memory had come back to him, and he could hold it back no longer.

"Aunty Jean, does Rachel still live with her parents? I mean, is she still, is she still…my girl? You see; I have something to confess to the both of you. I wanted to do it all along, but Rachel wanted to keep it a secret until I got back home."

Everything he wanted to say for the last few days came pouring out in one big breath. Since his sense of timing was still a little off, he thought he was telling them something they did not know.

"Uncle Zeek; Aunty Jean, I'm asking for you forgiveness. I went against our agreement, and the agreement I set up with Mr. and Mrs. Zook too. I went past the agreement of engagement, and Rachel and I got married the night before I left. Now, with all that has happened to me, I can't imagine what kind of trouble I put Rachel through. I know she must have told her folks by now."

Ezekiel looked at his nephew with forgiving eyes. He thought: *At least he has one part right; he can't imagine!*

chapter

EIGHTEEN

Rachel woke the next morning still thinking on what Bobby said about his make believe friend. There were a lot of things she had to learn; so much she did not know about mothering. Having younger siblings to care for, taught her a lot of things, but the responsibility of real parenthood was a different matter. Mamm prepared such a nice Sunday dinner last night that Rachel decided not to bother her at breakfast. She would fix some good hardy oatmeal for her and Bobby. He did tend to have a sweet tooth at times, so she topped the oatmeal with brown sugar, raisins, and a few shakes of cinnamon. She sat thinking for a few minutes about her family. Moses was going to be twelve in April, and being in the eighth grade, if her parents were still practicing the Amish faith, it would have been his last year to attend school. The good thing in that is, he would be there to help Daed on the farm. *I feel sort of bad that Elizabeth and I were born first. It would have been wonderful gut if the boys had come before us, but God knows what He is doing.*

Rachel wanted to talk with her mother about Bobby's statements. She went over to the main house with her son, as was her usual routine by now. Mainly it was to help her Mamm with the morning chores, as a good daughter ought. Most times she waited until after the boys went off to school. This would be a short school week because of Thanksgiving Day coming up on Thursday. The boys still had a half-day of school on Wednesday. When the kitchen was prêt near redd-up, they had time to take a break. Anna Zook fixed a cup of tea, and some buttermilk biscuits (left from the morning meal) for her, and Rachel. Rachel took a quick look-see at Bobby stretched out in the (now) too small cradle that once belonged to her brothers, and went back to sit at the table. Anna listened to Rachel's concerns, but couldn't help but think they were a might premature for worrying over. Having raised four children of her own, she had experienced children who had very vivid imaginations, and a few who even had an imaginary friend.

"But Mamm, what about him calling me Mommy, and the little girl having the same birthday as his?"

"Oh… I don't know. I'm not an expert at these things, but the way I see it, a child's imaginary friend has to be just like he, or she wants them to be, or as close to them as possible. It's either *that*, or they're the exact opposite."

Anna set her teacup down, and lovingly touched the back of her daughter's hand.

"Rachel, don't fret over this little episode. There will be many more in his life, and maybe a lot more serious than this. You're a new Mamm. You'll see him grow out of one thing, and into another. Who knows what the good Lord Heavenly Father has in mind for him. Ain't so?"

Rachel took another sip of her tea. She agreed with her lips, but something down inside her heart sensed this was more than met the eye.

Back at the hotel, the Miller's made a call back home to Tina. They knew she would be on pins and needles until she heard from them. The man in the hospital was indeed their Robert! Tina cried tears of happiness all over again. There was something more. His past memory had been restored, but it was the three years he missed as Robert Williams that he wanted to know about. The doctors suggested that the Millers stay over a couple of days and ease information to him a little at a time. He was so unaware of all the things that had taken place, and he was full of questions. He was anxious to get back home, but sadden to have to say goodbye to the McAfees. Norma Jean asked Tina to find a way to get the word to the Zook's early the next day, if she could. Her mother emphasized that they should be alone. Then, the Zooks could decide how they wanted to break the news to Rachel. Mrs. Miller said it had to be done first thing in the morning, because she was sure the newspapers, television, and radio would release their broadcasts as soon as they were notified. She said even though Robert was a grown, mature man, his mind was in a fragile state, and the doctors would guide them as to how much information he could handle in a setting. One of the two doctors would be in the room with them over the next two days to monitor their conversation, and Robert's responses.

Early the next morning Tina Marie drove her folks car down the road to the Zook's, but parked it down near their turn off. The night before was sleepless for her. She worded, and reworded what she would say to them. Mrs. Zook was surprised, and a little concerned to see Tina Marie that early in the morning. Her eyes met Tina's in a worried stare. The boys were just leaving for school, and she invited Tina Marie in. Tina explained that she had something important to tell her, and her husband together. Anna Zook offered her some breakfast, and she accepted since it was still on the table, and she hadn't fixed any breakfast for herself. Anna called to her husband who had just left the table to collect a few things for the work-day ahead. When he came in, Tina didn't want to hem and haw, so she got straight to the point. She gave them the basic information she knew about Robert. Needless to say they were overcome. They had plenty of questions, but not wanting to prolong the time, just in case Rachel came over; she would leave that to one who when he came home, could best answer all their questions…Robert.

Tina said it was suggested that they share about Robert being found, but not the part about his coming home this week, because that may not be a certainty. At any rate, the two families were still expecting to share Thanksgiving dinner together as planned. Tina knew she must go. With her mother being out of town, a good part of the shopping, and preparing for the holiday meal would now fall on her. She also was expecting to have a visit from Rachel before the end of the day. If she were able to get most of the shopping done by then, maybe the two of them could talk, and work on preparing a dish ahead of time that could be refrigerated; like the filling for the sweet potato pies.

⮞⮜

Bill wanted to post a letter to Mrs. Lapp to see if she had any news about Mr. Zimmerman's property, but he thought it best not to stir up any suspicion about his being in Walnut Creek. The local mail carrier would surly read where the letter was post marked from. He could just as well ask Mr. Yoder about the property. Maybe he had a better knowledge of the property, and could tell him more than she could. He almost forgot how things worked around the Amish community. To ask a woman about what was considered to be man's business was a '*no-no*'.

Bill had not heard a word about Robert being found, or being looked for since he had come back. He wanted more than anything to get out of that one room he lived in at the motel. He had enough of apartment life, and one room living. He wanted a home, a place to call his own. Actually, he wanted to be blessed with a wife too. He was tired of living alone, and not having anyone to share things with at the end of the day. Living the way he was, he had nothing to offer…nothing to attract a wife. At least, owning a home, and a piece of land would be somewhere to start. *Maybe then he could approach Katie.*

~~

Ezekiel and Norma Jean answered many of the questions Robert had to ask as directly as they could, but he had so many questions. Under observation by both doctors, who were on hand at different intervals to chart his temperament, they were cautioned to keep their answers as direct, and short as possible. The doctors did not want Robert to become overwhelmed with small details. Of course, not living in the Zook household, the Miller's could only share from an outward perspective what had occurred over the past three years with Rachel. Most of it had not been good.

Robert was told that as far as they knew, Rachel was still his wife. No annulment had taken place. They gently informed him of Rachel's situation, and let him know that he was a father; but no other details were offered. His wife could better share with him whatever else he needed know. They told him that Rachel was living in the 'Dawdi Haus' with their son, so there was a private dwelling where he could live with his family, but that their home was always open to the both of them as well. There was so much more he wanted to know, but they said they would share more on their next visit.

By the time they left the hospital that afternoon, the news of Robert's reappearance had surfaced to the media. When the first floor elevator doors opened, Ezekiel and his wife needed more than the one liaison assigned to them.

Cameras were flashing, microphones were being shoved in their face, and commotion was everywhere. Among the crowd were two more officers who had been appointed as escorts for them. Each of them grabbed one of their arms, and pushing through the huddle, escorted them to a waiting vehicle. Someone behind them was reminding the reporters that this was still a hospital zone, and if they could govern their selves accordingly, a news conference was scheduled for 3:00p, and Sergeant Baise from the United States Army, along with the patient's doctors, would answer all of their question. With that going on, the Millers were told they were not going back to the hotel right away, but were going to take a detour out to visit the McAfee's.

⌒⌒

Rachel had come over to help her Mamm redd up after breakfast. Out of the corner of her eye she saw the figure of a man headed out from their turn off. It was her Daed. Strange, she thought. Where could he be headed this time of morning? If anywhere, he should be headed out to the barn. Rachel came in the back door, and stopped in the mudroom to remove Bobby's heavy sweater. Walking into the kitchen she found her Mamm sitting at the large table having (what she surmised to be) a second cup of tea. Rachel surveyed the area. Anna Zook had dawned her work apron, but nothing had been cleared away. Bobby ran to the table, arms waving in the air.

"Groot moeder, Groot moeder." (Grandmother).

Anna Zook reached for the tike, and put him on her knee.

"Hullo, my lieb. Bist du gut boy de mariye?"

"Jah Gommy".

"Ach, how about a piece of scrapple, and a buttermilk biscuit with apple butter?"

Bobby was smiling from ear to ear. His grandmother looked at Rachel. She gave a nod of approval, and said:

"Mamm, where was Daed going this time of morning?"

"Oh", she replied, making her voice calm and steady. "He's going to the shanty to call Ben. He wants to see if he can come over to help him cut some wood today, if he can spare the time."

Actually, the call was to see if he and Elizabeth could come over right away for support when they shared the news with Rachel about Robert. Abraham took his time walking back home from the phone call, and Anna stretched out her clean up time with her daughter, hopefully, to synchronize with Ben and Elizabeth's arrival.

chapter

NINETEEN

Mrs. Miller was able to telephone her daughter from the McAfee's house. Tina told her everything went well with Mr. and Mrs. Zook (at least she hoped it did), but she was not sure if Rachel knew yet. Her mother said she could now call her brother, and the pastor to let them know the news. She wanted to be sure they knew about it, before the broadcast came over the TV news; and that would be pretty soon from the looks of things. The McAfees said they weren't that surprised to find out that Robert was married. They knew he was either married, or engaged because of the ring he wore. That's why they gave him the name Jacob. They were already bracing themselves for his goodbye, but were hoping he would not forget them altogether, and would come back for a visit.

On their way back to the hotel, the Miller's were told to expect a few straggling reporters who wanted something extra for their paper, or news broadcast, to earn them some extra brownie points. Sergeant Baise was to meet them at the hotel, and he would keep them from being pestered by the press. The driver apologized for the inconvenient, but explained that in 1963; it wasn't a difficult thing for the media to find out that a Negro couple was staying in a well-known hotel in the city.

Back in the hotel, he relayed to them what was said to the media about Robert. Nothing was mentioned about his being married, or even being engaged. They thought that was better left alone. He did say, since Robert was making such a remarkable recovery, and all data on him had been cleared, so far as Uncle Sam was concerned, there was no reason to detain him past tomorrow afternoon. His doctors had contacted a clinic in Strasburg, and arranged for his check ups, and visits. His Veteran's pay would be kicking in soon, and all his medical expenses would be taken care of. The last thing was that the Army would be flying them back home in a special jet. It would arrive at the Cleveland airport, and from there they would be driven in a limousine, straight to their front door in Walnut Creek. The same privilege would be afforded to Robert when he was ready to return.

As anxious as Robert was to go home, he decided to wait until Thursday. He wanted to say a proper goodbye to the folks who took care of him, and treated him like their own son. Besides, before he left, he had a few lose ends to tie up concerning the other house. He knew he couldn't do it himself, but he would get his friend Steven, who helped him out from time to time, to finish up what needed to be done. He had a little money saved back from the part-time work he did, and he would see that Steven got paid for finishing up for him. It's funny, Robert thought, how God works. Here I am for almost three years not knowing who I really am, and all the while, because I never received my last pay from the Army, it's been in an account drawing interest. Not only that, they're trying to decide since I wasn't AWOL, if I'm entitled to my full three years of service pay. I thank God I'm getting my life back, but most of all that I won't have to go home to my family empty handed.

⁓

Donna was hurting all over. Her heart, her mind, and her spirit were in agony. *Why, she kept asking God? Why?* Donna tried to sooth herself with her *rights,* and legal justifications, but nothing she came up with could block out what her pastor said to her just a few days ago. She had been a Christian long enough to know the Word of the Lord when it came to her, and maybe that's what was bothering her. Pastor Quincy may not have understood all what he said to her, but something he said in the message let her know that it was truly the Will of God speaking to her. *'I have loaned to you'.* Why did God have to say, *that I have loaned to you?* Why couldn't He have said, *that I have given to you?* When she thought about it in her heart, she had to admit; *aren't all children on loan to us from the Lord? We are to be just good stewards (parents) over them for Him.* Then, a Bible scripture came to mind. Psalm 127 says something about children being a reward from the Lord, and Proverbs 22:6 says, *we're given children to train them up in the way of the Lord*. Hopefully, I've done that as best I could in this short time. But then, she continued thinking. There was the other part of what Pastor Folks said. *"I'll give you the desires of your heart"*. While she was deep in thought, the ring of the telephone interrupted her musing. She wasn't sure how many times it had rung, and rushed to get it before the caller hung up.

"Hello." It was Pastor Folks.

"Oh, hello Pastor Folks."

"Good evening Sister Donna. Am I interrupting anything?"

"No. No sir, not at all. As a matter of fact, I was just thinking about you."

"Oh?" His voice had a pleasant questioning about it.

"Oh, what I mean is… I mean what I meant to say was, I was just thinking about what you told me on Sunday. It's something that won't leave my mind."

"Look. That's why I called you. I was going to wait until Wednesday, but that's the day before Thanksgiving, and I didn't want to interrupt your family's time together. It's just that you seemed a little upset when you left my office, I was concerned, and wanted to make sure you were all right."

He tried to keep his voice of personal interest in this woman out of his *pastoral duty* voice, but it was challenging.

"Well to tell you the truth, I'm not doing that well."

"Oh. Is there anything I can do to help? After all, I feel kind of responsible in a way." His pastor voice was speaking, but his inner man was yearning: *say yes, I can help, Please say yes.*

"Pastor, I don't want you thinking for one minute that what you told me wasn't from God, because it was, and I feel I ought to share some things with you that might help to clear the air. But, I would have to speak with you in person."

He was trying to remain calm. He couldn't believe his ears. The *Holy Spirit* reminded him that it was Pastor Quincy who was coming to her rescue, **not** the man Quincy. A still small voice said: *Don't let your good be spoken of for evil!*

Collecting himself, he said:

"Okay sister Vaughn, how is your schedule today?"

"It's pretty much clear this afternoon, except, I have to work second shift at the hospital. It's not my usual time, but I'm covering someone else's shift. Hey, I know. If I go in a little earlier around three O'clock, do you think you could meet me at the hospital?"

"I think that can be arranged, just say where."

"Well, lets see. Come in the main entrance, and I'll meet you in the lobby. We can go to a private family waiting room area on the fourth floor. After I've shared what this is all about, there is a patient I want you to meet. He may be going home tomorrow, and I believe he kind of ties in somehow with the message you gave me. If that's true, I'll need your advice about a decision I think I have to make."

"Alright. I'll meet you in the lobby at three. Goodbye."

Donna put the receiver back on the cradle. She stood there for a moment thinking how easy it was to talk to Pastor Quincy Folks, and a slight smile cornered her lips.

∽∽

Rachel's family surrounded her with love and affection. One never really knows how they will feel, or react to news of this nature. You think because you've been praying by faith, and you've rehearsed it over and over again in your mind, you know exactly how you will feel, and what you will do, but you don't! Something flashed through Rachel's mind. *Oh my Lord. Over the past few years, I've thought about what I would say the day my husband and I were reunited, but not once did I think about what I would say to my children (my son, about his real father). Maybe that's because...I never imagined in my wildest dreams I would have my children back again. The reunion was always about the two of us.* She never even realized she said; *...my children back again.*

Rachel was full of questions that her parents could not answer. She wanted to go right over to the Miller's, but was informed that Mr. and Mrs. Miller were with Robert, and Tina had gone to do some shopping since most of the meal cooking would now fall on her. Rachel asked Elizabeth if she wouldn't mind keeping an eye on Bobby. She needed to go back to the Dawdi Haus for some quite time, and meditation. When she got there, she got the picture of Robert, and the *'Blue Waltz'* cologne out from her hope chest. She sat on the bed and traced the outline of his face with her finger. Then, out of nowhere an agony worked its way up from the pit of her stomach and into her throat. Before she knew it, she was on her knees before the Lord.

"My lieb, my love, my love, you're alive!" She began to praise the Lord. Thank You my Lord. I Love You with all my heart. Thank You my God. You are my refuse and strength. You have been so merciful to me. I'm no one special, but in Your righteousness, and faithfulness, You thought of me. You answered my prayers, and You closed up the open womb in my heart"

Rachel wiped her face with the end of her blouse, and pulled herself up on the bed. *When will he arrive? Did they say? Will it be today, or tomorrow, this week? When?* "Help me Lord", she was talking out loud. If it's longer than two days, I'll have to go to him. I don't know what to do. I know. I'll go over to the Miller's and stay there until he comes. No. I can't do that. What about my son? I'll have to wait. I've got to pull myself together." She spotted Robert's photo on the floor. Rachel picked it up and held it to her chest. "My love, my love." *Should I keep your picture out, and explain to Bobby who you are? No, it's too soon. That will only confuse him.* Rachel calmed herself down, and decided the best thing to do was to keep busy. She washed her face with a cool face cloth, and went back to the main house. She asked her sister if she could spare enough time to help her redd-up the Dawdi Haus for her husband's homecoming.

chapter

TWENTY

Robert signed himself out of the hospital Wednesday morning. His plan was to spend the rest of the day with Mr. and Mrs. McAfee. He would spend one last night in his old bedroom, and leave for Walnut Creek in the morning. When he called home that evening, luckily his uncle answered the phone. Robert let his uncle know he would arrive late Thursday afternoon, Thanksgiving Day, but asked him not to tell his aunt. She would be worried to death the whole time until he got home. As far as she knew, his plan was to be in late that evening, or early the next day. Robert then asked to speak with Tina. She had always helped Robert with his secret meetings with Rachel, and he needed her help one more time. After his dinner with his other folks, Robert went to bed early, and this time when he dreamed his reoccurring dream; the lady who turned to call his name had a face. It was Rachel's.

∾ ∾

There was more business at the local grocery store on the Wednesday before Thanksgiving than at Jonas Yoder's shop, but they remained open to sell a few kitchen utensils and such that the womenfolk needed for their big dinner. The store would be closed on Thursday. Since the Yoder's were Amish, it was a very unusual thing for them to invite an outsider to their home on a family day like Thanksgiving. Bill could only surmise that with his being alone, and no family around, that Mrs. Yoder had compassion on him, and talked her husband into inviting him to dinner. He eagerly accepted, glad for the chance to sit with Katie at their table. This was just the opening he was looking for.

Back at the motel, Bill was anxious to find the listing for Mr. Zimmerman's farm in *'The Budget'*. He also brought the local newspaper. He wanted to see if they listed the realtor who was handling the property, and what the asking price was. Maybe he would begin to make some inquiries about it on Friday. Who knew, if all went well, he might have a place to call his own before Christmas. He wrote all the information down on a note pad, and put it in his wallet. He turned on the television, and went to the microwave oven to heat up the TV dinner he'd brought on the way in. Bill really wanted to stop by the Strasburg Diner, but it still was too chancy.

The broadcaster was announcing a list of events that would take place beginning Thanksgiving, and lasting through the Christmas holidays. Then, he stopped far a special news bulletin. The screen went to a video recording of the Millers coming out of a hotel followed by news reporters, and cameramen. Bill rushed over to turn up the volume. At first he thought it had something to do with Civil Rights, but it didn't. Then, without notice, a still photo clip of Robert filled one side of the screen. The caption moving across the bottom read: MISSING SOILDER FOUND AFTER THREE LONG YEARS.

...."Yes", the anchorman was saying, "It appears that the missing solider you see here in the photo is one Robert Williams of Walnut Creek, Ohio, who has been missing for the three years. He has been found. He reportedly was robbed, beaten, and left for dead in an abandon house somewhere near Lancaster, Pa. over three years ago. The head injury he sustained caused Amnesia, and the elderly couple that found him has been taking care of him all this time. He has been living under the assumed name of Jacob McAfee. What an amazing Thanksgiving family reunion this will be for the William's family." Bill stood frozen. The microwave bell must have gone off, but he never heard a thing.

Both the Zook, and Miller households were up early on Thursday morning. After the evening news had aired the night before, calls came in to the Miller's from all over the area. Rachel had gone over the evening before, not because she knew anything about the broadcast, but because the Millers had returned, she hoped they could tell her news of her beloved husband. While she was there, the news aired again. Her heart jumped when she saw the photo of Robert flash across the screen. It must have been an older photo, because it looked very much like the one he sent to her. After that, Norma Jean sat down and had a talk with Rachel. She told her all she knew about his situation. She said he had changed a little; more grown up she supposed. Robert confessed to them about he and Rachel's secret marriage, and because his memory went back that far, they felt it only fair to let him know that because of their honeymoon night; he was a father. However, they only mentioned Bobby. The doctors cautioned against giving too much information about his missing years being pushed on him all at once. Anyway, there were some things that were private between them, and should only be shared by his wife. Mrs. Miller said he wanted to come home right away, but thought it of great importance that he said a proper goodbye, and thanks to the McAfees who had kept him. He would probably be home late Thursday night, or early Friday morning.

Mrs. Miller, Tina Marie, Rachel, and her mother planned every good thing they could think of for their first Thanksgiving dinner together as a family, but in their wildest dreams, they never expected to have the added blessing of Robert being found. Between the two families they had enough food to feed a small army. Dishes from both family cultures had been prepared. The menu consisted of baked turkey with cornbread stuffing, Dutch goose (pig stomach stuffed with a mixture of sausages, potatoes, bread and seasonings), sweet corn, buttered noodles, chow chow, mashed potatoes with giblet gravy, succotash, home made yeast rolls, chocolate pecan pie, sweet potato pie, and shoofly pie for the children. And, if that weren't enough, because friends, and church members had heard the news about Robert coming home, they too were dropping off prepared dishes for the family.

The Miller's dinning room table (even with extension leaf in) would only accommodate the eight adults, so, in order to seat the children, they had to borrow a folding table from the church. It would be set up just inside the archway of the kitchen. This was the first time the Zook's ever heard of a *children's table.* Up until now, a separate table set aside for someone in the Amish family meant they were shunned. *That's not a bad idea, Anna thought, a children's table. It'll give the little ones a chance to talk on their own level, but they'll be close enough for adults to monitor what they say.* The mealtime was set for 2:00pm, a little past the regular lunch hour, but well before the usual hour for the evening meal.

Several calls came in during their dinner, and Mrs. Miller apologized. This would not have been a normal thing for them, except they knew the news of Robert's return had reached several homes by now, and they didn't want to ignore any neighborly calls. Tina Marie sat in the chair closet to the living room where the telephone was, so she could answer the calls without her parents having to leave their meal. Rachel was on pins and needles. She dropped her fork a couple of times when the phone rang. Any of those calls could have been from Robert. Tina kept the conversation short with 'well-wishers' on the other end of the line. She promised to deliver their message to her folks as soon as she got off the phone, which she did do.

Another officer was filling in for Sergeant Baise on Thursday. He got Robert to the airport, and made sure all his other connections were secure for his arrival. On the drive from the airport, Robert thought back on the odd visit he had the night before he left the hospital. It was from the nurse who was over his radiology test. She brought her pastor along with her. When they first entered the room, he thought they were husband and wife. The nurse said she heard he was being discharged the next day, and was glad he was progressing so well. What seemed odd to him was that the well wishes spoken from her lips, did not coincide with the sadness that was in her eyes. The pastor was a pretty cool guy, and Robert promised to look him up when he came back for a visit.

His mind turned back to the task at hand…getting home. He could only hope that Tina had done what he had asked her to do. While riding in the back seat of the limousine from Strasburg to Walnut Creek, Robert thought about how blessed he was, and how much he loved his family. But, as much as he loved them, the first face he wanted to see was Rachel's. The first arms he wanted to fall into were Rachel's, and the first lips he wanted to kiss were the lips of the sweet Amish girl he fell in love with. The passing scenery became very familiar, and triggered his memory even more. Robert instructed the driver to stop short of his house and let him out. He grabbed his small satchel from the seat, and working his way on the inside of the thinning thickets, he maneuvered towards the rear of the barn. He hunched down to let himself in the unlatched doors, *thank you Tina, he said to himself.* He walked nervously through the dim lit barn, and opened the door to his little office room. Wow! Tina had everything ready. The Coleman heater had warmed the entire room. He stood for a few minutes, and looked around. So many memories flooded his senses.

Robert hung his jacket on the back of the chair at the desk, and sat down. He took a couple of deep breaths, and picked up the receiver to the telephone on the desk. He put the phone to his ear, and heard the hum of dial tone. Tina was right. The line was still connected. Robert tried to imagine what Rachel would look like. "Well here goes", he spoke out loud. The plan was to dial the house telephone. Hopefully Tina would get the phone on the first, or second ring. When she answered, he would hang up, that way she would know he had made it in, and was in the office. If her folks asked who it was, she would simply say, they hung up when she said hello. Which would actually be the truth. After that she would mosey over to Rachel, and tell her that yesterday a letter came for her from Robert. She was to say, she didn't want to leave it lying around in the house knowing that so many people were coming in, so she took it to the barn, and put it in the desk drawer.

Rachel's heart was pounding. She couldn't think of a reason to excuse herself to go to the barn alone, so Tina asked if they could leave for a few minutes; she had something she wanted to show Rachel in private. The girls got their coats, and left together. Tina waited in the clearing between the house and the barn until Rachel reached the door. Robert discarded the gum he was chewing when he heard the outside double barn doors open, and a few seconds later the latch on the office door lifted. Rachel was so anxious to get to Robert's letter; she thought her eyes could have been deceiving her. Sometimes coming in from direct daylight, and the cold into a warm dimly lit room plays tricks on your eyes. It takes them a few moments to adjust. Robert moved out from behind the desk towards his wife. She's beautiful! He seemed to be moving in slow motion. Rachel shook her head back and forth hoping to clear her vision. *She was not dreaming. She was not having a hallucination.* This was for real! It was Robert, her Robert. He caught her in his arms, and pulled her to his chest lifting her feet from the floor. They clung to each other crying, and saying each other's name over and over again. Their lips met in smothering kisses. Their salty tears mingling with more kisses. Yes, sweet, sweet kisses. Lost in his embrace, memories of their honeymoon night surfaced in her mind. They both began to tremble, and had to compose themselves.

"Robert, I can hardly breath."

He knew it was true, but didn't want to let her go.

"Rachel. You're not a dream anymore. You're real. You are really real!"

"Jah. T'is me. It's me, and you're here in my arms. My own true forbidden love."

"Not any more. I'm going to hold on to you, and never let you go my darling. He tried to talk between kisses. Your fears were right. I almost didn't return to you."

They both were exhausted, and needed to step back from each other.

"I have so many questions, so much catching up to do."

"Don't worry about that love. You're home, and that's all the matters for now."

They knew they had to go to the house, and Robert had to greet the rest of the family. He turned out the heater, and grabbed his coat from the back of the chair. Rachel watched her husband as he moved across the room. This man was taller, and stronger than the man that left three years ago, and she liked it. Robert turned out the light. He gave his wife one more kiss, and said:

"Rachel. I'm so sorry for all the terrible things that you had to suffer through alone, but now that I'm back, as God is my witness, I promise to turn every ounce of your past sorrows into pinnacles of joy, or my name isn't Robert J. Williams, and *that J.* stands for Jacob!

"Ya mean to tell me that your middle name really is Jacob?"

"No. It's Johnathan." He replied, smiling. "I can see we still have a lot to learn about each other. It's just that because I was given that name by the McAfee's in my time of refuge, I intend to keep it as part of who I am."

Standing outside in the cool fresh air, he pushed the one side of the open barn door back on its hinge, then he took Rachel by the hand saying:

"Come my *fraa*, let's go get started on the rest of our lives."

chapter

TWENTY ONE

It wasn't that Bill did not recognize the stranger's face in the crowd that day. It's just that the news bulletin confirmed what he already knew in his heart when he left the Lancaster train depot three years ago. His exhilaration was spewing over. He had to do something to calm himself down. In the past, he would have reached for a cigarette, or maybe have taken a drink, but that was the old Bill. Temptation is always lurking around. He just didn't want to give it any opportunities to stay. He had one more day before visiting the Yoders, and he didn't want to stir up any old skeletons. This was the kind of good news you shared with close friends, and family, except he didn't have any. Bill had to laugh at himself, as he thought of the Bible story turned backwards. Instead of the *Prodigal Son,* he was the Prodigal Father come back home. He had to wonder if his son would receive him back. Bill took his mind off the immediate news to think back to when he first saw his son's face in the crowd. *Lancaster*: of course, it was Lancaster.

Knowing what might be the course of the day for Robert set his mind at ease. At least he knew there was no chance of their running into each other. They would be headed in two different directions. There weren't many places open on Thanksgiving Day, but Bill wanted to bring a little *thank you* something along to give to Mrs. Yoder. Had he been an Amish family member, and a woman, he probably would bring some kind of baked dish, or dessert for the meal; but since he wasn't, he didn't. He did remember some mannerly teachings from his child-hood days, and did not want to arrive empty handed. He decided to stop at the A&P supermarket to see if he spotted anything that would be adequate. He meandered up and down the aisles hoping something would strike his fancy. Nothing caught his eye. On his way out of the store, Bill went down the greeting card aisle, and saw something at the very end that caught his attention…fresh flowers. He was surprised to see brightly colored potted plants in the month of November, but what did he know. The saleslady said they were fall blooming perennials. Bill chose what looked like bunches of miniature purple pedal daisies with bright yellow centers. They were perfect!

◦◦

On her way to work the next morning, Donna reflected on her visit with Robert Williams. All had gone well. She got to know little pieces of him while he and

Pastor Quincy talked. That was the first time Donna got to observe Pastor Folk's personal mannerisms, aside from their short talk in the waiting room area. Listening to Robert's conversation, she could denote a certain amount of maturity in him. Pretty good she thought for a guy (she guessed) to be about twenty-one, no more than twenty-two years old. She was able to pick up on his religious convictions, and could hear how much he loved his wife, and missed his family. In saying goodbye, Pastor Folks offered for him to stop by the church the next time he was in town. He said he would be sure to, because he wanted to bring his wife and son to meet the folks who took care of him for these past three years. Donna walked Pastor Folks to the elevator, and thanked him again for going out of his way to oblige her.

Thankfully, her evening at work was going along smoothly and quietly. In the midst of going about her duties, Donna thought about what Robert had said about bringing his son to meet the elderly couple. It was evident he didn't know about a daughter. She was glade she didn't ride down in the elevator with Pastor Folks. Her office was on the next floor down, yet she waited until the elevator went all the way down, and then she pushed the button for it to come back up. Later, before her shift ended, she thought badly about not inviting him to Thanksgiving dinner. *Oh well,* she thought, *even though he has no family here, he is the pastor. He probably has lots of invitations from the church members.* When it was time to go, she thought about how crazy her schedule was this week. She had to work from four to midnight today, and from seven in the morning until three on Wednesday. She had Thursday off, but had to work Friday and Saturday.

Donna left the building with other workers whose shift ended the same hour as hers. Several groups walked up to the employee's lot together. When she got to her car, she got in and locked the door before putting the key in the ignition.   It was just one of those safety precautions she always took. She turned the key, but nothing happened. *'What'?* Maybe I didn't turn the key hard enough, she thought, so she tried again…nothing. Was the battery dead? Her headlights *were* a little dim. She turned the key off. Now what do I do? By then, everyone else had pulled out of that part of the employee parking lot, and she was by herself. She didn't want to chance going down through the gates, and across the lot alone. She began to pray asking God for direction. Just then, she spotted one of the hospital's motorized security vehicles going down the row behind her. *Maybe the battery isn't gone down completely.* She honked the horn twice, and saw the three-wheeled vehicle turn her way. The security guard rode her back to the building to use the telephone. Donna explained to her mother what happened, and said she needed a ride home. Mrs. Vaughn said Donna's father couldn't come because the Optometrist had put those drops in his eyes, and he had to ware those funny looking sunglasses home today. He was instructed not to drive alone for the next twenty-four hours. She said she could come, but that meant getting Lizzy up to bring her too, because she didn't feel comfortable waking her husband to ask him to keep an eye on Lizzy.

Donna didn't want her mother going through all of that trouble. She told her not to worry, that she knew someone who could bring her home. She felt awful having to call anyone at that time of morning, but she reached in her purse and took out the card pastor Folks had given her last Sunday. The voice on the other end of the line sounded alert. Maybe she didn't wake him after all. He told her to stay put, and not to worry about anything; he would be there in about twenty minutes. She apologized again before she hung up, and told him she would be downstairs in the lobby at the front entrance of the hospital. He told her she didn't have to apologize; it was his pleasure, and then hung up the phone. While walking to the front of the lobby, she thought about what pastor Quincy said. *He'd be here in about twenty minutes. She knew it took at least half an hour to get to the hospital from her house, and she thought he lived out farther than that, closer to the church.*

Quincy Folks could not believe his fate. This was incredible! He was doing his little happy jig. He knew it was far from doing a *'holy dance'*, even though he was praising the Lord. He let out a "Wahoo, Thank you Jesus!" Earlier, he was not able to sleep, so he decided to turn on the radio. He thought if he sat, and read a book while listing to soft music, he would get sleepy, but he didn't. He couldn't get Donna's situation off his mind. Now that he knew the story behind the *'Word'* from the Lord, he understood why it was so upsetting to her. Quincy was stumbling all over himself trying to get dressed. On his way to the car, he was grinning like a Cheshire cat. He had been sitting in that chair wishing that he didn't have to wait until Sunday to see Donna again. Turning onto the highway, he praised God saying: "You not only answer prayer, but sometimes You're down right speedy about it. Hallelujah!"

Donna was taken back a little when Quincy came through the double doors in the lobby. He looked different. He was wearing a pair of jeans, loafers, and a Ban Lon shirt that fit in all the right places. He may not have been trying to show off his physique; but *'wow', she thought. All that has been hidden under pulpit robes, and Sunday suits.* Immediately, she felt a wave of embarrassment for thinking of a man of the cloth in *that* manner. The conversation on the ride home was a bit strained, and Donna felt somewhat responsible for it. However, this time she did invite him to Thanksgiving dinner, and he readily accepted. Quincy parked in front of her house, and when she started to reach for the door handle, he was already saying,

"Here, let me get that for you." He hopped out of the car, and ran around to her door.

"Well, here we are, he said. Now, sister Vaughn, how will you get to work (he looked down at his watch) this morning?"

"Oh, that's not a problem, I'll just use my folk's car."

He seemed to be thinking. "Are you sure that's a good idea? I mean, with it being the day before Thanksgiving. Suppose your mother needs to run to the store at the last minute to get something she forgot?"

(He continued) You would be at work with both of the cars."

Um, hadn't thought about that. He's right. He could see the thought turning around in her head, so he took the liberty to venture on in boldness.

"Look, why don't I take you to work in the morning. No use getting your parents up that early. And, besides, if they waited up for you tonight, (he looked over his shoulder and nodded to a light still burning in an upstairs bedroom window), you wouldn't want to wake them up that early to take you back to work".

Before she could refuse his offer, he rushed on with his plan.

"Tell you what I'll do. I'll call one of the mechanics from the church to come by the hospital tomorrow, and check over your car while you're at work. Carlton's a real nice guy, and he'll give you a fair price if any repairs are needed."

Pastor Folks could feel an objection rising, so he held up his hand as if to say 'stop'.

" I won't take no for an answer. Say yes." He had a slight smirk on his face.

"All right. Yes."

"Good. What time shall I pick you up?"

"How about around 6:30? We'll try and miss the rush hour traffic."

"Sounds great. I'll be here at 6:15."

"But, Pastor 6:30 is just fine."

"Not for me Sister Vaughn, he said, flashing her another smile. If I'm getting up that early in the morning to take you to work, the least you can do is allow me to swing us by a drive-through for my morning cup of coffee. Good night my lady."

And with that said, he hopped into his car, and drove off into the night.

⌒⌒

Dinner with the Yoders was very beneficial. Many of the old ways came filtering back to Bill's mind. Some traditions, like the silent grace prayer at the beginning of the meal were still observed by the Yoders. However, because of so many outside influences brought in by the youth, some traditions had been relaxed. The mealtime, usually silent, held some conversation. It wasn't *chatty,* like the English, but some pleasant talk was carried on. Of course, it could have been because this was a special celebration meal, or maybe because he was an invited guest. Bill was not sure. He was able to obtain information about Mr. Zimmerman's property, and Mr. Yoder seemed pleased of his inquiry about it.

Alice Yoder, though usually somewhat of a talkative person herself, was noticeable quiet during the meal. Maybe she was more attentive to the eye exchanges going on between her daughter, and *Mr.* Bill Williams. She was in no wise upset about it; as a matter of fact, she thought it wonderful *gut!* Except for one thing. He was an Englischer. She wanted her Katie to get married again, but to an Amish man, not an outsider. When the evening was over, Bill thanked Mrs. Yoder for the wonderful meal, and out of the blue, directed his next question to Mr. Yoder.

"Excuse my bluntness sir, but would it be fitting if I was to ask Katie to walk with me out to my vehicle?"

Everything stopped! Mr. Yoder went on as if nothing out of the ordinary had just been said.

"Oh...I don't see why not Mr. Williams, but hadn't you best be asking that of Katie herself?"

"O Yes sir, he said, I guess so."

Katie looked at her Daed, and he gave his head a nod of approval. She was *plum purple embarrassed,* but that did not stop Bill from moving across the room to take her arm. They stopped at the pegs in the mudroom to get her heavy shawl. Bill placed it over her shoulders, and they went out the back door. They were scarcely off the back stoop when the kitchen erupted in hard laughter, and through a chuckle Mr. Yoder said,

"Well Mamm, fancy, or not; you's got to admit one thing, he's mighty bold."

Gathering some empty plates from the table, and in a make pretend huff, she replied: *"That's for sure, and for certain!"*

chapter

TWENTY TWO

Rachel was grateful that the Thanksgiving gathering at the Miller's was such a success. She introduced Bobby to Robert, letting him know that he was a family member of the Miller's, and a very special friend of hers. The evening ended around 6:00pm, and the Zook's took Bobby home with them. Upstairs in Robert's old room he and Rachel began their discussion about their living arrangements, and what would happen from this point on. They were legally married, but had to admit, they were virtually strangers. The three years they were absent from each other had changed the both of them, but not their love for each other. Yet, they didn't want to prolong the time before they could come together as husband and wife. They were in challenging circumstances. Rachel just couldn't have a man show up, and start living in the Dawdi Haus with her and Bobby, and Robert didn't mind staying with his folks for a few days, but anything past that time, his flesh could not promise to be faithful. Besides, Rachel didn't dare put one more family situation before her father to take to the bishop. While they tried to figure things out, Robert agreed to help his uncle and Mr. Zook with whatever they needed to be done around their properties. At least he could burn off pinned up anxiety, and get to see Rachel, and Bobby every day.

By Monday, the whole county was abuzz with the news of Robert's return. Reporters came out to the house for interviews, and some even came to the church to take pictures. That was another reason the couple had to be careful. Rachel and Bobby attended church with the Miller's, and sometimes the Zook's came. Fortunately, there was another Caucasian couple there, and a Hispanic family that attended also. That way Rachel didn't stand out like a sore thumb. The Zook's decided not to attend church with the Millers the Sunday after Thanksgiving. They mostly still wore their traditional Amish garb, and although the pastor, and parishioners were use to them being there, reporters might find a reason to keep digging into why an Amish family was attending a *Negro* Baptist church. This was not the time to inflame gossip around Robert's return home, nor the Amish community. They took the drive up to Brewster, calling for a taxi. Anyway, they wanted to spend a little time with Ben and Elizabeth.

Christmas was four weeks away, and Donna was more afraid than ever. She was pretty sure of what she was hearing in her heart, but called her friend Louvain Bell anyway. She also wanted to update her on what had been happening over the past couple of weeks. She called her office, and Louvain put everything aside to listen to her friend. She was shocked! In all her experience as a child placement supervisor, she had never heard of anything like this happening. Her professional advice to Donna was that nothing she told her negated Donna's legal right to declare Lizzy as her child. However, morally, and off the record, the decision was left up to her own conscience, but personally as a friend, she wouldn't want to see her hounded down through the years by a decision she made in haste, or out of fear. Louvain suggested that maybe she could talk to her pastor, or someone like that, who could help in giving her counsel. Donna having left out the personal information surrounding her and Quincy Folks, knew that's exactly who she was trying to avoid talking to. *Although, she didn't know why. Well, to be perfectly honest, she did know why.* She had three encounters with him in one week (four if you count Sunday), and she was pretty sure he was interested I her.

After dinner last Thursday evening, he indicated he would like to see her socially, but she did not give him an answer. She only told him, she would have to think about it. Then, yesterday in service, she looked up several times, only to make direct eye contact with him. *My God,* she thought, *I hope no one else is noticing this.* But, she was wrong. At least three other people took note of what was going on, the church secretary, Mrs. Vaughn, and a certain parishioner named Rita, who had designs for Quincy Folks; though he had no interest in her.

Pastor Quincy greeted the congregation from the pulpit. He said he hoped everyone had a wonderful Thanksgiving, and to keep those in mind who were still traveling back home. He asked us to pray for *traveling mercies.* He opened a portion of the morning service for those who wanted to give a short testimony about what they were most thankful for; putting emphasizes on the directive *short.*

Had that been just one week ago, I probably would have gone up to share an array of things I was thankful for, but today, I sat glued to my seat. My world had been shaken! Too many things had happened at just the right time to be accidental. I even shared everything with my parents, and I wasn't ready to accept what they were feeling, because I was feeling the same thing in my heart. In my flesh, it is a hard thing to accept, but I know the Holy Spirit is right. *I must return Lizzy to her natural parents.*

I must have been in deep thought, because service had ended, and I hadn't even stood for the benediction. How long had I been sitting there in a world of my own? Did I even hear the sermon? All of a sudden I felt the gentle touch of someone's hand on my shoulder, and turned to see pastor Quincy standing at the edge of the pew. He leaned in, extending his hand of greeting.

"A penny for your thoughts." Then he said, "No, I'll go one better than that. (A smile crept at the corner of his lips.) I'll give you *that* penny, and you *don't* have to have dinner with me today, if you can tell me what my sermon was about."

Oh, my goodness. I'm busted! I did muse through the sermon. Feeling a flush of embarrassment cross my face, I managed to apologize.

"Then, I take it we have a dinner date for this afternoon?"

What in the world! I didn't give him an answer on Thanksgiving when he asked to see me socially, and now he's busting a move on me in church. I don't know why this man is interested in me. I just don't know if I'm ready to date a pastor.

"Say yes, (he was saying) because here comes Mrs. Daily, and she's going to be wondering why I've been holding your hand all this time."

Donna didn't realize that her hand was still in his. He kept a planted smile on his face while he kept speaking through clenched together teeth.

"Quick, say yes, so I can let go of your hand. If you don't, the both of us are going to have a lot of explaining to do."

"Okay. Yes."

He dropped her hand, and said in a pleasant tone of voice that was a little louder,

"Yes, sister Vaughn. I can see the importance of that matter. Let me check my calendar, and I'll call you this evening if that *date* is clear."

Standing, he greeted Mrs. Daily who had reached their pew by that time, then turned and walked across the sanctuary to his office.

≈≈

Bill thought he had everything figured out. He would first visit the Miller's, and then the Zook's to reveal his true identity. He wasn't shunned when he first got out of prison, but he came close enough to it. He knew he couldn't come back to Walnut Creek and live, so he left, and gave up his right to the family's land. Times had changed since the old days. Females could inherit the family property, so he thought his sister's would want it. He wanted the Miller's to know there would be no claims coming from him against them for ownership of the property. All he wanted to do was come back to the community, and live as God was directing him to.

That was his original plan, but now that Robert had been found, he might have to alter it. Suppose Robert wanted to purchase the Zimmerman place for himself to be close to the Millers. Suppose he hated his father for deserting him when he was nine years old? He knew absolutely nothing about his son. He could only guess that Robert was not married, because the news said nothing about a wife, and family. He did surmise one thing; that he and Robert favored each other very much. That's what caught his attention that day before he followed him to the train depot, and evidently, that's what caught Mr. Zook's attention the other day over at the Zimmerman place. There was another important matter hanging in the balance. Ever since he returned, he had considered becoming Amish. When he finished with the property issue, and paid his visits to Zeke, and Norma Jean, and the Zook's, he was going to approach Mr. Yoder on the matter of becoming Amish.

chapter

TWENTY THREE

Robert had only a few acquaintances before he left home: his family, the Zook 's, and the folks at the Diner. He knew that Mr. Parker must have heard of his return by now, and he wanted to pay him a visit. He just wasn't sure if Rachel wanted to go along. He knew that Mr. Zook had planned to meet with bishop Daniel Zook (his brother) on how to handle the matter of he and Rachel. Abraham Zook, and his family were shunned for openly confessing their salvation through Jesus Christ. So, technically they were no longer members of the Amish church. However, because Rachel married during her Rumschpringe, and had not yet made her kneeling vows to the church, she was not shunned, but because she did not pledge to become a life-long member, she was considered to be outside the church; unless she wanted to repent of her sin, and come back to the Faith. Abraham wasn't even suppose to talk to his brother, but there were ways of making request, and seeking input on things that would affect the Amish community as a whole. It all boiled down to Robert and Rachel being seen together as a married couple.

Rachel came up with the idea of her riding in the back seat of the car when Robert asked her to go into Strasburg with him. There was nothing against the Amish taking taxies to town to handle business and other things. Robert had to laugh. It was almost too ironic to be funny. Here they were in the middle of a Civil Rights movement, and Rachel was the one who had to sit in the back seat.

It was the last of November, and the weather was mighty cold. The warm car was a welcome relief from her parent's closed-in buggy, even heated with the hot bricks. Personally, Rachel didn't care where she sat, as long as she was with her husband. This was the first day they had time to be alone with each other. The stores and businesses were all decked out in their Christmas array. She had almost forgotten how festive and colorful it could be. The gloomy weather, the bareness of the trees, and the bleak gray skies put such a damper on the winter months.

Robert parked his uncle's car in the parking lot. He quickly jumped out of the driver's seat, and opened the back passenger door for Rachel. There were two other cars in the parking lot; he recognized one of those as Mr.

Parker's. His face broadened in a smile at the fact that Mr. Parker was still driving his '54 Chevy. Glancing in the café window he saw that two tables and a booth were occupied. The other customers must have been walk-ins. Robert decided they would walk in together, and took Rachel's hand. This time it was Rachel who was concerned about them being a *mixed* couple; though you could hardly tell, because Robert was so fair skinned. His brown locks had even lightened some; she guessed it was because of his working out in the sun. Linda looked up when the bell attached to the door gave a ding-a-ling. She had just cleared a booth, and was on her way back to the kitchen with the gray plastic tub container when she took a second look at the customers. *Oh, my God! It's Robert.* Linda nearly stumbled with her load of dirty dishes. The clattering noise caused Mr. Parker to look her way.

He moved from behind the counter, grabbing a towel on the way, to wipe his hands. The men embraced each other, and patted each other on the back. Mr. Parker kissed Robert on the right cheek, and then on the left. Tears streamed down their face. In their excitement and greetings they were talking over each. Mr. Parker stepped back, greeted Rachel, and the threesome slid into the cleared booth. He told Robert he heard the news broadcasts, and hoped he would pay him a visit before too long. Mr. Parker said he hired a guy about two years ago, and he was working out pretty good. After a year, he had given him the night manager position, but if Robert was looking for work, he always had a job waiting for him at the diner. Robert thanked him, and said he wasn't exactly sure what he was going to do, or even if he would be staying in Walnut Creek very long. Rachel was shocked to hear him say that. They had not fully discussed all their plans for the future, but leaving Walnut Creek was something that never came up.

Linda came over to take their order. His old boss told him their meal was on the house. Since there were no more customers in the Diner at that moment, they sat and talked for a while. Mr. Parker noticed the ring on Robert's finger, and asked, "Are you two...?" Robert chimed in before he finished asking the question.

"Yes, but no one knows except for our family's, the Amish bishop, and you. So, if you don't mind, mums the word until we go public with it."

Mr. Parker smiled, and nodded his head. Although he was thinking to himself, *they must not know that ever since they came through the door,* **WE'RE MARRIED** *has been written all over their face. If they don't want anybody to know, they better keep hidden.* He left the table when their order came, but before he left, he told Robert about the stranger who came in the Diner last year. He told him the man looked so much like him; he could have been his father.

⌒⌒

The bishops, and the elders had two inquiries before them; they just had no idea the two people involved were related, until after the discussions began. The first was concerning Robert Williams, and his marriage to Rachel Zook. Though the situation had many twist and turns, most of the resolve had been predetermined. Rachel was just a teenager in her second year of her Rumschpringe when she ran off and got married. It was without parental consent; however the parents had agreed to an engagement. Being as Rachel was a married woman, and it could pretty much be concluded that she became pregnant on her wedding night, she had not sinned against God.

Next, because she had not taken her kneeling vows before the church elders, she was not considered to be a member of the Amish church, and was now considered to be an *outsider*. As for her interracial marriage, that was not a *spiritual* issue for that council to vote on. Even though this was the first of its kind to happen in the district, there were no similar circumstances to compare it to. The *Ordnung* promoted certain guidelines for outsiders to adhere to, in order to join the Amish community, but so far as they knew, this did not apply to Rachel's husband. It was decided that this was not a decision for the Church, and their ruling was to be silent on the matter.

Mr. Yoder arranged Bill's meeting with the elders, and the bishop. He was completely honest about his background, and previous dealings with the law. The younger elders, and deacons had not been acquainted with Johnathan Holfman's parents, but Daniel Zook had known them well. He commended Bill for wanting to come back to the Faith, and they set a time for his proving to begin. His overseer would be Jonas Yoder, since he was the one to most likely see him on a daily basis. Though it wasn't mandatory at the moment for him to do so, if he wanted to begin wearing the Amish clothing, he could. It was said that somehow wearing the traditional garb helped to remind folk what they were pledging to become a part of. Bill's studies were to be with the bishop, but would not begin until after he studied the Ordnung. He would also have to purchase the Ausbund (the Amish hymn book), and the *Martyrs Mirror;* which held the writings of many martyred forefathers of the Mennonite and Amish faith.

One of the most surprising things that came to light in the interview was that Rachel's husband, and Mr. Bill Williams were father and son. Bill asked for this information to remain silent until he himself had the opportunity to reveal it to Robert. Never the less, it left the bishop's council in an interesting state of affairs. Mr. Williams was born by Caucasian Amish parents. His son was born of an interracial union between he and Mr. Zeke Miller's sister. However, the lifeline is in the blood of the father. Robert may have his mother's DNA, but he has his father's blood. This was the second time in the past year that issues of this nature crept into the discussion of the elders. What makes a person Amish? Is one Amish because he is born to Amish parents? Is he Amish because he is raised practicing, and living the Amish lifestyle? Or, are they Amish because he, or she took life long vows to serve in the beliefs of the Amish faith? These were the questions that rose out of their meetings. *Why is it,* Daniel Zook pondered, *that these things come when I'm serving as bishop for the district, but not only that; Why do they always seem to emerge from my own brother's household?*

chapter

TWENTY FOUR

Bill felt he had to move fast to do the things he needed to do. With Robert's face being plastered all over the TV, and newspapers, people were sure to notice some resemblance between the two of them. First, he would clear things up with Mr. Yoder. If he hoped to get anywhere with his daughter, Bill wanted Mr. Yoder to know what he shared with the council. His second visit was to visit the Miller's, but on his way, he had to stop by the Strasburg Diner, and talk with the owner. He may be able to tell him some things about Robert he needed to know. Bill pulled up in front of the Diner, and parked. Out of the corner of his eye, he viewed a nice couple coming out of the Diner, and they walked to the parking lot located on the side of the building. He fished in his pocket to get change for the meter. He thought a quarter would give him more than enough time, but then he remembered how talkative the owner was, and he put in fifty cent.

The lunch crowd had died down. The couple he saw leaving must have been the last of it. Good, because he wanted to be able to talk with the owner without interruptions. He took a booth, and picked up a menu. Mr. Parker headed his way with a glass of ice water. He got to the booth, and stopped in his tracks. This was just too canny to be true! Bill saw the look on his face, and asked him to have a seat.

"You must remember me", he said?

Mr. Parker was ready to say something, when Bill cut him off.

"Evidently you do, from the look on your face. Look, I'm not going to beat around the bush. My name is Bill Williams, and I'm Robert William's father."

"Yep. I kind of figured that was the connection between you two."

"It's no accident that I've come back here. I mean here to Ohio. The Miller's actually live in the house that once belonged to my family." He rushed on to say. "Oh, I'm not here to cause any trouble, or anything like that. I want to go back to Walnut Creek and live, but I've got a lot of apologizing to do to a lot of people first. Ya see, I want to join the Amish church, and I want to go into things with a clean slate. Even before I showed up here last year, I was praying for my son's return. I just didn't know he was going to show up now. Well, I was remembering how much you thought of Robert and all, so before I meet up with him, I thought you could tell me a little bit about him."

Bill realized he had become the talkative one. Mr. Parker could not resist the temptation to explain why he had *that* look on his face.

"If you want to know the reason why I was so dumbfounded when you came in, it's because that last couple who just walked out of here was your son Robert, and his wife."

"What? His wife! You mean he's married?"

"Yep. He married an Amish girl who lived next door to the Millers."

"You mean he's married to Elizabeth Zook?"

"Nope. Not her. He's married to Rachel her sister… got married the day before he went to the Army, and we never laid eyes on him again until he showed up here last week…been gone three years."

"What, you've got to be kidding!"

"Nope. It gets even better than that. He never knew he was a daddy 'til the Miller's went up to Lancaster a few days before Thanksgiving to identify him. Rachel was going to let him know she was expecting a baby when he got back home from basic training…'cepting he never came back. That's when he got that *Amnesia.*"

Bill could not believe his ears. The whole thing was too incredible.

⚬⚬

Donna had no idea where Pastor Quincy was taking her. She still hadn't convinced herself about dating a pastor. She felt guilty about her feelings, but she wasn't sure she wanted to be seen out in public with him. Donna was so nervous. She didn't know what to do on a date with a pastor. Then, she had to laugh at herself. *Who am I kidding!* I wouldn't know what to do on a date with any man. It's only been *four* years. Now she was a little perturbed, she had no idea what to wear. She couldn't dress down too casually; after all, it was *still* Sunday. Then again, she didn't want to look all *suity* stiff, like one of those *First Ladies's* coming from a convention dinner. She made a couple of drawn snooty faces in the mirror, the way she thought some uppity person would look. That brought a smile to her face, and she relaxed a little. *If only I knew where we were going.* The telephone rang, and it was for her.

"Hello, sister Vaughn, this is pastor Quincy. I see that my calendar is clear today, so would about four o'clock be okay?"

"What? Who is this?" What calendar?

Quincy let out a small chuckle. "I was just being true to the statement I made as Mrs. Daily was approaching us, and I didn't want it to be said that I was not a man of my word."

"Oh, I see." She made a goofy face, and rolled her eyes.

"Anyway, I thought you would like to know what I had planned for our outing, so you would not worry about what to wear. I know how particular ladies can be when it comes to something like that."

"Thank you pastor, I appreciate your sensitivity."

"Do you like the Theatre?" He was hoping she would, because that was one of his favorite places to go.

" Oh yes I love it, but it's been ages since I've gone."

"Well, I thought we'd go to a dinner theatre. It's not far from here, only about a six, or seven-mile drive. I'm sure we won't run into any of *our* church fellowship there today. Most of them are eating near shopping centers, or at the buffets. So, I guess the fashion for today is *casual*, or do you ladies call it *dressy casual?*"

"Thank you. I'll try to find something appropriate to wear."

"I've never seen you in anything less. See you at four."

Donna placed the receiver back on the hook. She gave in to a little smile that curved the corner of her lips, and looking up to the ceiling said, "Lord, this man is too good to be true! He calls to give me a heads up on where he'd like to take me, and evidently he's been paying attention to how I dress. I hope he is for *r-e-a-l*." She had a good two hours before her date, so she went to spend some quality time with Lizzy.

⌒⌒

On the drive back from the Diner the seating arrangement was the same. Rachel sat in the back seat. In their visits together during the past week, Rachel shared everything with Robert, even the adoption of his other child. She had never before seen that much hurt in a man's eyes, but how was she to know these things, when she was only sixteen? She had no clue of the world, or the experiences it had to offer. She still was concerned about what he meant by being uncertain about staying in Walnut Creek, but she withheld the urge to ask. They had almost reached Sugar Creek, when all of a sudden Robert quickly pulled the car over to the side of the road. He put it in park, jumped out of the vehicle saying, "Hang it all!" He opened the door where Rachel was sitting, and said, "Rachel, get out." Her eyes were as wide as saucers. She didn't know what was going on. What had she done? "Dog gone it, if I'm going to take this any more. Get out of that back seat, and get up front where you belong!" He took her arm, and walked her around to the front passenger door. When he opened it, he nearly shoved Rachel in. "I want my wife sitting up front beside me where she belongs, not in the back seat. And, *Bump* any body who has a problem with it." He got back in the car, pulled out onto the road, and didn't say another word the rest of the way home. Rachel remained silent too. She looked his way a few times trying to visualize this new Robert. He certainly had no fear of taking authority when he needed to.

They arrived at the Zook's backyard, and Robert came around to let Rachel out. He took her by the hand, but when she started to move, he didn't let go. He stayed fixed right where he was.

She turned to look at him. "Rachel, (he said in a calm voice) you are going to go in the house, and ask your Mother if she can watch Bobby for a couple more hours. Then, we are going over to the Dawdi Haus. There may be some things we're waiting to hear by tomorrow before everyone knows that we are husband and wife, but I guarantee you this one thing, that when we leave the Dawdi Haus this afternoon; there will no longer be a question in your mind that we *sure–nuff* are married!"

⊂⌒⊃

Already the house seemed empty and lonely for the McAfees. Robert had called them since he had been gone, and his friend had dropped around a couple of times to see if they were in need of anything. He was finishing up some sort of project that had to do with the house, so they did not interfere. Robert said how much his missed them, and wished he could visit before the Christmas holiday, but there were a lot of impending circumstances surrounding he and his wife's situation, and he desperately needed to stay put until everything was in order. Of course, they understood only to well. But, Robert (their Jacob) said he would try and call them at least once a week if not more often, until he could arrange for a visit.

chapter

TWENTY FIVE

Bill knew he had some challenging days ahead, and the only way to come out the victor was to forge forward. On his visit to the Diner, he got the Miller's telephone number from Mr. Parker. Bill must have paced the floor several times before he dialed the number to his brother-in-law's house. He was praying that Robert would not answer the phone when it rang. He heard a woman's voice.

"Hello." It was Norma Jean.

"Hello, she said again, is anyone there?"

"Uh, hello. Is Ezekiel Miller home?" He knew his voice had a little quiver in it.

"Yes he is. May I say who's calling?"

Bill was caught off guard. He didn't know what to say. He thought for a second, and then said:

"Well, if you can just tell him it's...it's someone who knows his family from years back, and I would like to come by to see him."

Mrs. Miller laid the receiver on the table, and was on her way to call to her husband when he came through the back door stumping his feet on the throw rug, to rid his shoes of the light show that had begun to fall. He thought it could get worse, so that's why he went out to put the truck in the barn. She indicated that he had a phone call waiting for him, so he came through the hallway, and reached for the phone on the living room stand.

"Hello, this is Ezekiel Miller."

"Hello Zeke, this is Bill... Bill Williams."

There was a pause of silence. Then he said: "Excuse me. Who did you say this was?"

"Believe it or not, it's me Bill Williams, Robert's father. I'm not dead, as some may have supposed. Actually, for the last few months I've been living up near Strasburg. I guess I've been trying to work up the nerve to come and see you. If you and Norma Jean will have me, I'd like to come out and talk to the both of you."

Ezekiel was still stunned. He held his hand over the mouthpiece, and gave a short explanation to his wife. She said it was wonderful, and to see if he could come for dinner. Bill said he would love to come to dinner. He explained that his original plan was to talk with them alone, and had no idea at the time he had planned to come and see them that his son would be found, and living back home.

"Well, if you've been reading the papers, or listing to the news, you'll know how unexpected it was for all of us.

Since he *is* home, let me have a little talk with him first
to get a feel of where he is on the matter, and I'll get back
with you. Is there a number where you can be reached?"

Bill left him the number where he could be reached,
and hoped for the best.

~~

Donna reflected on how wonderful her date was
Sunday evening with Pastor Quincy. At first she was a
little nervous, but when she warmed up to him, their
conversations went quite smoothly. She found out that
they liked many of the same things. Christmas was big on
both of their list. They talked about their childhood days,
and at certain points, she even forgot she was out with her
pastor. She had to admit, he wasn't *that* bad, he seemed
like a regular kind of guy.

On the drive back to the house, he brought up his
concern for Lizzy and me, and wanted to know if I had
come to any decision. When we reached my house, we had
not finished our conversation, so we stayed parked there
for a while. Even though he had been in my parent's home
on more than one occasion, I considered this as a *first* date
with him, and inviting a man in after your first date with
him, was definitely a *no, no.* I told him I decided to allow
Lizzy to be placed back with her birth family. He said he
knew that was a difficult decision for me to make, and he
would assist me in any way that he could. I jokingly said,
I could use a little of your strength if you have any to spare. At
that time, I started to feel a weepy moment coming on,
and thought it best to say our goodnights.

It wasn't really late, but I knew I wanted to get an early start on getting in touch with Child Services the next morning to give Louvain my decision. Pastor Quincy walked me to the door. He took my hand, and I thanked him again for such a wonderful evening. He smiled at me and said:

"Does that mean I get to see you again?"

Shyly, I told him yes, I would like that very much. He leaned in to give me a quick kiss on the cheek, (the *holy kiss* type) but still; I could feel the tenderness in it. He waited for me to open the door. When I was inside he started to leave, but turned back to say:

"I'll tell you what, if you'll drop the *pastor* part when we are seeing each other socially, I'll drop the *sister;* agreed?"

I agreed, and he gave me that amazing smile of his, and said goodnight. On my way upstairs, I stopped half way and thought to myself, *Are you crazy, dating a pastor? Are you ready for this girl?* "Maybe", I said out loud.

The next morning Donna decided to keep Lizzy home from Pre-school. She wanted to spend some time with her, and search out an easy way to explain to her that she may soon be going on a long trip. After breakfast, Donna got out her picture diaries, and she and Lizzy sat on the living room sofa. Donna read, and pointed out several things to her daughter. They laughed at the funny pictures, and Lizzy asked questions like; who is this Mommy, or how old was I in this picture? At one point she got quiet, and looking up at her asked:

"Mommy, where are pictures of the little boy I know?"

Donna wanted to think she was speaking of one of the little boys from the Pre-school, or someone in her Sunday school class at church, but she knew it wasn't, because this had come up before. All she could think to tell her was that he was with his Mommy, and his Mommy probably had his pictures in her own scrapbook. Of course, knowing something of the Amish, she knew that was not the truth. They don't take, or keep photos. Then, Donna took a brave step, and asked Lizzy if she would like to visit her little friend one day. (She wasn't sure if asking that would do more harm than good)

"O yes Mommy. Yes." Lizzy's eyes were twinkling, as if her imaginary friend was really real. Donna hoped she had not made a big mistake.

⌒⌒

When Robert returned from his outing with Rachel. His demeanor was very upbeat. Norma Jean was in the kitchen when he came in. She knew a light snow had been falling for a while, but noticing his head she thought; *"His hair looks wet. If he's been riding in the car most of the time, why does his hair look as if he's been out without a hat on?"* She quickly put the thought aside. There was something more important to discuss now. Robert's uncle and aunt said they needed to speak with him in private. He thought it was the heart to heart talk they had not gotten around to since he returned. He felt great about his future, and was just waiting on the next move of the Lord.

Robert could not believe his ears. If this was the next move of the Lord, he was completely thrown off track. *His father was here. Here in Walnut Creek?* He always had the feeling that his dad was not dead, and he knew that maybe some day he would come back, or at least he would come looking for him...but, today? Now? Robert started to feel anger mount in his spirit, but he knew that was the trick of the *Enemy.* Why should he be angry about the very thing he had prayed about for the last twelve years? He had to realize that God was answering his prayers. So, why get angry about it? The Holy Spirit reminded him that he *too* had disappeared out of his family's life for several years, but when he returned, the family rejoiced.

His father was going to join them for dinner. In the meantime, Robert sat in his room pondering over all the happenings of the last three years.

The policeman in the crowd, and then again at the train station, the man Mr. Parker said came in the Diner last year; they were all connected. Yes, he thought, I know exactly what my father looks like. Maybe he had a feeling of who I was *that* day, and knew he had to find me to make amends. Robert began to pray:

"Dear Lord, whatever it was that took my father away and kept him from returning all these years, let it be buried in the depths of the sea. Remove all guilt and shame from his life, and any anger, and hurt from mine, in Jesus' Name Amen"

Ezekiel answered the doorbell when it rang. The man standing on the front stoop was the man who married his sister twenty-two years ago. Without speaking tears filled Ezekiel's eyes, as did Bill's. They hugged each other in unspoken silence, knowing that each of them had the same person's passing in their mind, and in their heart. The brother's-in-laws gave each other a hardy pat on the back, then, Bill greeted Norma Jean.

"Welcome back home" she said. This is Tina Marie. I don't know if you remember her or not."

"Yes I do, but the last time I saw her, she was about seven, or eight years old." He moved forward to shake her hand.

Just at that time Robert descended the stairs, and walked in the hall entryway near the living room. The two men stood gazing at each other for what seemed like a long time. Mr. Miller broke the silence.

"My God! It's like looking in a mirror that goes back twenty years."

Bill and Robert fell on each other's neck weeping. Norma Jean pulled the hankie from her apron pocket, and dabbed at her eyes. Bill pulled the handkerchief from his back pocket, wiped his eyes, and then blew his nose. Mrs. Miller asked everyone to please come sit in the living room; that dinner would be on the table in a few minutes. Bill sat in one of the *Queen Ann* chairs. He didn't want to hold up the dinner, but he had come on a mission, and he wasn't going to pull up a chair to his brother-in-laws table until he had asked for their forgiveness. Tina, and Mrs. Miller excused themselves to the kitchen, so the men could talk. She was sure her husband would let them know when they were ready to eat.

⟨⟩

Bill wanted to do everything decent and in order. He knew the Zook's were under the *Bann,* so he made arrangements through Mr. Yoder, who talked with the bishop, to have a special audience with Abraham Zook. Bill was trying to clear up all discrepancies of the past, and for any ongoing relationships in the future. Since his son was married to Rachel, he wanted to assure Mr. Zook, (who knew him as Johnathan Holfman) that his legal name is Bill Williams. It was the name he was married under, and his son's last name (on his birth certificate) was legally that of Williams. On the way back from the visit with the Zooks, Bill asked Mr. Yoder if it was still proper for him to see Katie during his 'proving'.

"Ach, proper or no, fancy or Amish, I've already given my agreement on that to the both of you's. I'll not go back on it now. Besides, (he said with a chuckle) neither one of you's is getting any younger." Bill was certainly in agreement with that.

chapter

TWENTY SIX

Pastor Quincy was attentive to Donna now more than ever. So much so, that she was worried that their relationship would be noticed by some of the church members. She really had to be careful. Carlton, the mechanic that Pastor Quincy sent to look at her car, said that one of the cells in the battery had dried up. He said letting it charge up with a *jump* would allow it to run for a little while, but he couldn't promise me how long that would do the trick. It would be my choice if I wanted to get a new battery, or not. Rather than be stranded somewhere on the road alone, I decided to invest the fifty dollars for a new battery, and be worry free. Now, my car was running just fine. Still, the next time I had to work second shift, Quincy Folks insisted on taking me to work, and picking me back up.

During the week Donna made an appointment to meet with Louvain Bell on the upcoming Friday. Pastor Quincy volunteered to drive her in his car. It was only a four-hour drive, or so to Strasburg, but he didn't want her to have to stop at a pay phone if anything went wrong. He was becoming a good friend, and the needed spiritual support in her challenging endeavors. On one of her lunch hours at work, she dropped in to see Dr. Al, and shared the things that had arisen out of the 'Robert Williams' incident. But, she was mostly concerned about this *friend* Lizzy had dreamed up. Dr. Westly said it was not uncommon for twins to share the same experiences, or to do similar things, like picking out the same clothing, or furnishings, even though they were miles apart, and had not consulted each other. Grant it, this was more prevalent in identical twins, or for those who were much older, but there were so many things the medical field did not know about the way brain messages work in twins. As an added note, he said it would be interesting to find out if the other twin was experiencing some of the same sort of thoughts. But, of course he said, that would be impossible, being that the other twin was adopted at birth too, and we didn't know his whereabouts.

It wasn't until Donna and Pastor Quincy arrived at Ms. Bell's office, and was questioned by the two interviewers, that she was told of Rachel getting her son back. Louvain said she withheld the information on purpose, not wanting it to influence any decision she was to make. After the others left the office, Donna became nervous about the interview. Pastor Quincy was sitting next to her across from Ms. Bell's desk. She let her arm drop by the side of the chair, and felt for his hand. Her hands were as cold as ice. He felt the touch of her fingers and enclosed his warm hand around hers, then gave it a gentle squeeze. Ms. Bell told Donna the next step was to get started on some paperwork. It would be easier this time around, because most of the groundwork was already laid. Primarily she would be reverting all of her claims on the original adoption papers. Depending on how quickly this was done, Lizzy could be back with her parents before Christmas. They had all the files they needed on the mother, and after Donna had placed her call the other day, a file on the father was being formulated. A caseworker and psychiatrist would be assigned to work with Lizzy and her family members, and her friend suggested that Donna seek counsel for herself as well. This was a very traumatic thing to go through, and it made Donna think of what it must have been like for Rachel.

"Don't worry, Pastor Quincy said, we'll see that she gets all the help she needs to get through this."

"Great." Louvain. said. "Here's a list of agencies, and self-help groups we often recommend. Maybe you can check to see if any of them are in your immediate area. Meanwhile, I'll stay in touch with you as much as I can. Remember, this kind of thing is never easy, but when you walk out that door, whatever decision you make today, has to be final."

"Okay, she managed to say. What happens after this?"

" Well, I'll pass these singed documents along to the staff who has charge of this case. After processing begins, the other party should receive a letter of intent from our office within the next ten to fourteen business days. They will have the first opportunity of response, and because we see no need for Lizzy to be caught up in the system, the letter will probably suggest an immediate transfer on a designated date, that is if they are in full agreement."

She waited to see if Donna had any more questions, or concerns. When she didn't, she stood and shook both of their hands. She told her friend not to worry; she believed everything was going to work out okay.

Outside the office door a wave of uncertainty flooded Donna's emotions. She began to weep uncontrollably. Quincy put his arms around her, and let her cry. He understood this was a very vulnerable time for her, and he was there to support her as a pastor, and friend. He stepped back, and handed her the hankie from his inside jacket pocket. Before they took the four-hour drive back home, they stopped in at a local Diner to eat and relax. It was a cozy, quaint little place. They ordered cheeseburgers, French fries, and large Pepsi's with lots of ice. Neither of them was very talkative, but each of them knew they needed to breath in some quiet time after that encounter. When they finished, Donna sought out the ladies room, and Quincy paid the bill. He took a quick run to the men's room, and left a tip on the table on their way out. He held the door for Donna, and then waved a 'thank you' to the old gentleman behind the counter. Mr. Parker smiled to himself. *Nice couple, but didn't notice any wedding rings. If they ever pass this way again, I'll check out their hands.*

chapter

TWENTY
SEVEN

Bill and Katie were not sure how to go about their courtship. Certainly, regular rules did not apply. They both were well out of their teens. They both had been widowed. Bill was a previous Amish/Mennonite, turned English, now practicing to become Amish, and Katie had been Amish all her life. He had given Robert his car (which he would no longer be able to use anyway, once he took his kneeling vows), and he didn't yet own a buggy. Were they only to court at night? Could they be seen together in the day? He didn't know what to do.

Bill was pleased that the Zimmerman property sale was going to come through for him. He used a good chunk of his savings, and pension monies for the down payment because he didn't want to have a large bank loan. It would have been different if he had a craft that could earn him a living, but when he left Lancaster, he had not thought of needing extra money. He had enough for him to get by on, but now that he was thinking of providing for a wife; he knew he'd need to earn extra money. Katie Yoder was not a youth, but she was sure not past the child bearing stage. Wow! *I never thought about fathering any more children at my age, but I guess Katie will want us to have a family. Maybe within my heart, I do too. It'll give me a chance to make up for something I missed out on doing the first time around... being a good father.*

For the three weeks Robert had been home, he spent more and more time at the Zook's. In an effort to get Bobby use to seeing his father's face, the day after Thanksgiving Rachel put Robert's photo on the dresser in her bedroom. She wasn't sure how much a three year old could grasp, but since the two households were joined, Bobby was picking up on Amish, and English ways. Rachel had dropped most of the heavy traditional Amish practices, but her parent's household still held to most of them. She encouraged his learning by repeating some words in both languages. That way he would learn Daed/Daddy, Gommy/Grandmother, and Grandy/Grand Pa. She always remembered to include "God bless uncle Zack" in his nightly prayers. As the weeks went on, she could see things becoming a bit smoother. Robert was about the place so regularly, it surprised her one-day when Bobby asked, "Where is Daddy? Is he coming home?" That was when they knew it was time for him to move into the Dawdi Haus.

Ultimately, Robert and Rachel recognized all the concerns that both sides of the family had for them, but in the final analyses, they were the ones who had to face whatever choices they felt best for their future. Because there was no telephone service at the Zook's, Robert had to go up to the shanty, or drive back to his Uncle's house to communicate with the outside world. He was grateful for the car his father had given him. Now, that his father would probably become Amish in the very near future, he would be the one needing a ride from Robert. He thought about a lot of things over the past few weeks, but the most astounding thing to believe was that his dad use to be a man named Johnathan Holfman, and his family owned the very house and property where his aunt, and uncle now live.

Robert kept any mail he was receiving coming to his Uncle's address. He didn't want to introduce too many changes in this short period of time, especially with so many things turning out in their favor. He was sure in his heart they were supposed to leave Walnut Creek, but he knew the timing had to be right. His mind kept going back to that little house he repaired for the McAfees. In the beginning he thought it was for them to rent out, but now his heart was thinking something else. The place was about a forty minute, or so drive west of the McAfee's house, and maybe a good half days drive from Walnut

Creek. He knew if Rachel got the yearning to see her folks, he could always pack up the family, and they could be there in six, or seven hours.

Lancaster County was another hour, or two east of where the McAfee's were, so if they wanted to see the big city, they could do that too. His decision would affect Rachel more than anyone else. She had never been anywhere that was more than an hour's drive away from Walnut Creek, but he was sure she would soften up to the idea when he explained how convenient traveling would be by Interstate Hi-ways, and car. Besides, he thought neither Ben, Elizabeth, nor the Zooks are active in the Amish faith, they could even take the drive themselves if they wanted to.

chapter

TWENTY EIGHT

The second Sunday of Advent Pastor Folks preached about Christ being our strength in times of our weakness. He reminded the congregation that the birth of the *Baby* fulfilled the promise, but it was the strength of the cross that brought us salvation. Donna felt the message was especially orchestrated to meet her need, but she figured other's probably felt it met their needs too. She was pretty sure that she was not being bias, but Pastor Quincy was a mighty good preacher. It was evident that he prayed for the members of their assembly, because it reflected in the delivery of his sermons. They were full of love and compassion. It was amazing to Donna how so many people could hear the same message, yet it could settled in individual hearts to meet them at their personal point of need.

Pastor Folks, and Donna kept their meetings private. Mostly, he visited her at her home. Her parents were aware of their relationship, but kept it to themselves. During the week after her meeting with Ms. Bell, one of the things she did was to ask Lizzy if she wanted to draw a picture of her friend. Of course, she knew she wouldn't be able to tell what the picture was, unless this three year old was gifted at drawing too! Psychologically, she hoped this wasn't a challenging thing to ask a child to do, because after all, Donna understood this person wasn't real. If Lizzy seems to be struggling with what she wanted it to look like, Donna thought, *I could help her with the drawing.* She can tell me whatever it is she wants me to draw. They started on the project, and it looked like any other stick drawing a child would make. Donna gave her daughter a black crayon to color his hair, and Lizzy handed it back. She told her that *that* crayon was too dark, his hair is brown, brown like hers. Then, Donna had to try and draw medium brown hair with large wavy locks. They ended up using the regular brown to color his eyes.

The day after that, a package came from the agency. It contained copies of all the documents she had signed, and another letter letting her know that the office had sent a letter to Lizzy's parents. The paperwork was completed, and a caseworker had been assigned. Home visits for Lizzy's parents could start as early as December 17th, however, the agency thought it best not to remove a child from their home this close to Christmas, and thought it better to wait until after the holiday season was over. Donna was to expect the transfer (removal) to take place after the first of the year.

⌒⌒

Rachel was sitting at her mother's kitchen table when Robert came in with the mail. He had been chopping wood to store in the barn for the winter months. He wanted to do as much as he could for both households before bad weather set in. Robert hung around for a few minutes to warm up with a cup of tea, and to give Bobby a horsy-back ride. Rachel opened the official looking letter. She was sure she was reading the letter correctly, but her eyes must have been playing tricks on her. Her hands started to shake, and her heart began to pound. *What the World!* Mrs. Zook noticed that something was wrong. She signaled to Robert. He put Bobby down on the braided rug. Rachel passed the letter to her Mamm. She got half way through the letter, and dropped it on the table. Robert could get nothing out of either one of the ladies. Mrs. Zook was crying into her apron. She pointed at the letter. Rachel kept saying: "Oh my God! O my God!" *What is it? Did somebody die? What kind of bad news was it?* He picked up the letter, and read as quickly as he could. What? He went back over the last part that read…
and, it is our official duty to notify you that because of personal reasons by her adoptee, Lizzy will be returned to you by that said parent at your request…on the assigned date above of January 2, 1964, but no later than January 3, 1964.

In their rejoicing, and crying, they had completely forgotten about Bobby until they heard him crying too.

"*Nee. Nee.*" Anna scooped the crying toddler up in her arms. "T'is gut news my lieb that makes up cry; *ain't so?*" She looked at Rachel.

"Jah, jah, t'is gut news indeed."

Rachel, and her Mamm were mixing their Pennsylvania Dutch with their English. So, everyone put smiles on their faces for Bobby. Rachel ran to the barn to tell her Daed. Robert took the car over to the Miller's. From there he called Ben, and Elizabeth. This must have been their Christmas miracle.

❧❧

Donna talked with Lizzy a few times about going away on a long visit. She explained that Mommy, and Pastor Quincy would drive her there, but they would not be able to stay. To encourage her, she told her she might be able to meet her friend; the little boy, but Donna was careful not to say that she would be back to get her soon. This whole thing wounded Donna's heart in the worst way. Her parents tried to help with the situation as much as they could, but it was just as hard for them as it was for their daughter. Donna told Lizzy over, and over again how much she was loved, and told her there was another lady who loved her just as much as she did. Donna showed Lizzy the picture of Robert she had cut out of the newspaper, and let her know that this man was her daddy. She kept the picture out on the living room table, and every now and then would say to Lizzy in a merry voice; "Are you going to visit your daddy, and your other mommy?"

Lizzy would go over and put her little finger on the picture, and say, ..."going to see my daddy."

Pastor Quincy was more supportive than ever. Donna came to depend on his strength, and his friendship. He called her twice a day, and sometimes she feared she was keeping him from his pastoral duties. In one of their conversations, she mentioned she hoped she didn't fall apart when it got down to *Zero* hour. Quincy told her not to worry. If that did happen, he would be standing right at her side, and if she felt like falling, she could fall into his arms. That's one of the mysteries Donna couldn't quite figure out about him. How could he be so strong and powerful in his convictions to this faith, yet, still be so loving and gentle when it came to his concerns about her? She didn't fully understand it all, but one thing she did know for sure...she was falling in love with him, and she never intended for that to happen.

⌒⌒

Bill was ready to move out of his small motel room. The day he signed the Deed to his new house, he looked into getting the diesel engines turned back on in his name. He called to have the propane gas tank filled in order to power the cook stove, refrigerator, and for the hot water heater for use in the kitchen. He had no furniture to speak of at the motel; no need for it, but when he went out to help Mr. Yoder move Zack Zimmerman, he had his eye on the house. He worked out a deal with Mr. Yoder to purchase the kitchen and bedroom sets. He paid them off, and Mr. Yoder agreed to keep them in storage for him until he moved. He ordered a closed-in fiberglass buggy, and was having it fitted with a few updated essentials he knew would be beneficial. It would be ready just in time for him to get some courting in with Katie before Christmas.

Bill's goal was to get moved before the second snow came in. He knew he and Aaron couldn't bring the kitchen, and bedroom sets over in the market wagon, so again he had to get permission to rent a van. Mr. Yoder thought it would be all right seeing as, technically he was not Amish yet. Alice Yoder knew this man knew absolutely nothing about the feminine side of setting up housekeeping. He had lived in apartments and motels for most of his life. *For pity sakes,* she thought, *something will have to be done about that!* She sent a note by Aaron to Anna Zook, asking if she could help her out with curtains, bed sheets, and a quilt. The note said: nothing fancy, just enough to get a bachelor settled in. She didn't want to put the idea in Anna's mind that Bill was courting, and let alone with her Katie. Alice was bringing a cane back sitting chair, some bath towels, and pillows for the bed. Anna Zook shared the news with Norma Jean. The ladies were giddy with excitement. Norma Jean brought pots, pans, a skillet, and cooking utensils. The word somehow got up the road a piece to Lillian Lapp, and she came prepared with table settings, canned fruit, and vegetables, fresh eggs, and produce for the refrigerator. The ladies took over, and by the time they finished, the place looked like a descent place to *roost.* They all had a good laugh about it later on, calling that day their *'Unofficial Bee'* Bee.

chapter

TWENTY NINE

Once word spread through the gossip grapevine of Rachel's miracle; that's what they were calling it, the *People* started to look at the Zooks in a different manner. Oh, they still were shunned, but lately when they went to town, the People treated them not so harshly. They were not supposed to be able to buy from the Amish merchants. Their neighbors were supposed to turn their backs on them when they came in, and the storeowners were not to sell them any goods. The Zook's did not break the shunning rules. When they went into shops, they took someone with them to pick out and pay for their merchandise, like the Miller's, to whom the Shun did not apply, or Aendi Mary who didn't care what the People thought about her.

Out of all that was happening surrounding their family, it was Robert, and Rachel who got most of the attention. Oh, not because of their interracial marriage, but because the People were curious about the *favor the Lord* that placed over heir lives. Most of them did not turn their backs, or leave the shops when they came in. They stayed, and even offered a smile. It was just about a week before Christmas, and the threesome, Robert, Rachel and Bobby, were shopping for a few things they needed for the holiday. It was the first time they had gone into town as a family. On the way home Rachel chuckled out loud.

"What's so funny", Robert asked.

"You would think we were Joseph, Mary, and the baby Jesus coming to Bethlehem, the way people were starring at us."

"Maybe I need to look through your eyes, because their stares gave me a different feeling all together."

They started laughing, and Rachel scooted over to lay her head on Robert's shoulder.

Pastor Quincy had his eye on Donna for almost ten months before their first encounter. But, for her their relationship was relatively new. He knew there was too much going on in her life at this time for her to be even thinking of marriage, be he knew he wanted to marry her. He loved her, and knew she was supposed to be his wife. They had to get through Christmas, because after that, a major turning point was coming in her life. He didn't want her to think she was always on the losing end of everything. Even in this, there was something positive. *If there was only a way to show her what the Lord was putting in his heart...*

Quincy purchased Donna's favorite perfume for a Christmas present, and had it store wrapped. He sought out gifts for Lizzy, and purchased one each for Deacon, and Sister Vaughn. He then, left the shopping center, and drove the couple of blocks to the jeweler's where he picked up the engagement ring he ordered for Donna. Mrs. Vaughn was very helpful in getting the correct size to him, and she was very good at keeping a secret. His plan was to spend Christmas Day with the Vaughn's. He had asked Donna to visiting with his mother and family over the rest of the holiday, while Lizzy stayed home. His mother lived in Wilmington, Delaware, not more than an hour's drive away. His younger brother and his family planned to come over, and they all would have a second Christmas celebration. Donna knew she needed to get away for a day or so, but meeting his family was a big step. She was thankful that Quincy had a good relationship with his mother. He was very busy as a pastor, but set aside time to call her almost every day. She remembered hearing him announce from the pulpit several times when he would be out of town visiting his family. He said if he were needed for anything, Mrs. Daily would know how to get in touch with him.

I could see where Quincy got his love for the joy of Christmas. His mother's house was decorated beautifully. She did it all by herself, except for some of the outside lights. There was Christmas in every room in the house, and not a Santa Clause, reindeer, of elf to be seen anywhere. Mrs. Folks showed me to my room, and jokingly said I could put the lock on the door if it would make me more comfortable being under the same roof with her *son*. She knew Quincy and I did not have an intimate relationship going on; evidently, they shared almost everything.

His brother brought the family over about an hour before dinner so we could open presents together. I was surprised that my name was on several packages, but I shouldn't have been. His family was just as thoughtful as he was. I had an additional present to give to Quincy too. I had already given him a nice leather wallet, and a box of handkerchiefs with his initial on them at my parent's house. It seems I was always in need of one of his, so they were sort of for me too. I brought a beautiful gemstone bracelet for his mother, and a large tin of homemade sugar cookies for his brother's family. The dinner was wonderful, and almost late because we had to wait until *Pastor* Quincy finished making his *famous* chestnut, cornbread stuffing! I was honored that he asked me to help him in the kitchen. I only wish I knew before hand, that it was only to chop the onions.

I had taken two days of my vacation time off for the Christmas holiday, because I wanted to save the rest of what I had left for Lizzy's trip back home. Since Christmas was on Wednesday, I took off that Wednesday, and Thursday. To give myself more time, I switched hours with a co-worker, so I could work second shift on that Friday. After his brother left, Quincy told his mother we would put away the food, and wash the dishes. I didn't want to seem ungrateful for their hospitality and kindness, but it had been ages since I *washed* dishes, and besides, I had just paid for an expensive manicure. Quincy must have seen the look on my face, and I saw a smirk forming from the corner of his mouth. He said he was just kidding. He knew all along he was going to load the dishwasher; he just wanted to see how I felt about *manual labor.*

When we finished in the kitchen, we got a cup of eggnog, and sat on the sofa admiring the tree, and it was so relaxing listening to the crackling logs in the fireplace.

"Pretty good isn't it? He said. Are you nice and comfortable?"

"Umm, Yes. It doesn't get any better than this."

And though, as if what I said fell right on *cue,* he reached in his pocket, and pulled out a small blue box.

"It could get better than this if you will say the right words."

He opened the box to reveal a beautiful diamond ring, and got down on one knee.

"Donna Vaughn, Will you marry me?

I was stunned. I didn't know what to say. I was completely thrown for a loop.

"Donna, I know a lot is going on in your life right now, but I don't want you to go through it alone. I want to be a part of whatever your future is. I want you to know, I'm here for you. Because; Donna I not only love you, but I'm *in* love with you. Will you do me the honor of becoming Mrs. Quincy Folks?"

"I...I... I don't know what to say."

"Say yes. Say yes."

Donna couldn't resist a laugh, remembering other times when he said those exact same words to her.

"Oh, Pastor Quincy, so what are you going to tell me now; that Mrs. Daily is on her way down the stairs?"

"Hey. You never know."

She looked into the eyes of the man she knew she was in love with, and knew there was only one answer to give.

"Yes, I'll marry you Pastor Quincy Folks. Yes, I'll be your wife."

He slipped the engagement ring on her finger, and rose to sit beside her on the sofa. He took his fiancé in his arms, and kissed her. This time, not on her cheek, though the kiss was surly holy.

Epilogue

It's amazing the way the Lord can intervene solving the enigmas of our lives. Sometimes we can't see our way past the next decision we have to make, and God already has it figured out. One thing I know; *For sure, and for certain,* is we have to trust God. He alone knows what lies beyond the bend. He will bring wholeness to all our brokenness, even to the pieces that seem impossible to bring together.

Take a look at Rachel and Robert. One never knows why we go through the struggles, and difficulties we go through, but if we hold out until the end, we'll see that God can work all things together for our good. True, it's hard for us to leave familiar territory, and venture into the obscure, but there's favor in being obedient to the promptings of God.

Robert moved Rachel, and the twins back to the little house where he encounter danger; not just once, but twice over the past three years. But, now it's an arch of safety for his family. They are not far from the McAfees who serve as another set of grandparents for the children, and they have a loving heart for Rachel, just like they would for their own daughter. The oddest thing happened during the transitioning of Lizzy. When the twins first met, they seemingly recognized each other. They ran and clung to each other like long lost friends.

Donna packed the photo scrapbook, along with Lizzy's drawing of her special friend in Lizzy's suitcase. She wanted Robert and Rachel to see how their daughter grew up.

~~

Bill married Katie Yoder when the next wedding season came around. It is so ironic to see how the hand of God was on Bill's life. Since Robert moved away, Bill hired himself out to the Millers as their orchard worker. He knew the orchard, because he was raised there. Ezekiel made him supervisor over the orchard. It was doing so well, he arranged for him to have a yearly salary that paid him even in the off-seasons. That allowed Bill to help all year round with both of the farms. Oh, yeah, last Christmas Tina Marie's friend from college came to visit her. I hear the Miller's think very highly of the gentleman, and if wedding bells are in the future, they won't be losing a daughter, they'll be gaining a son.

Moses is growing like a weed, and is able to do more heavy work around the farm. That's not to say he'll be doing it for long, because he's still interested in finishing high school. After that, he wants to attend the local college to get a degree in electronics. It'll work out just fine since Bill is considered to be family, and helps out at both places. Ben ended up helping out at the hardware store with Mr. Yoder, and speaking of Ben; I hear that he and Elizabeth are expecting another wee one very soon.

Pastor Quincy announced his engagement to Donna at the 'Watch Night' service. Donna wanted to wait until spring to get married, however Pastor Quincy persuaded her to have their wedding on Valentine's Day. The congregation (except for a few ladies) thought the idea was so romantic of him, but *he* knew there were some other pending circumstances that just couldn't wait until spring... and he was one of them!

Walnut Creek had gone through many changes over the years. I guess every community does. I even hear the bishop has mellowed some, but not enough to the end the *Bann* on his brother. No matter, whatever befalls us; we raise our strong flags of faith, and plant them firmly in the Word of God. Yes, I love the changing of the seasons, but now with added years, I realize it's not just the seasons of nature that change, but also the seasons in our lives.

22705742R00129

Made in the USA
Charleston, SC
27 September 2013